VICKY'S ESCAPE

By

Gary Wheaton

Other Books By Gary Wheaton

Urchin

Saving Blackrock

Hitchhikers

Worlds Apart

Down Up North

The Old Man And The Hooker

New to North Carolina, Victoria Trent has killed a football hero because the town idol was trying to rape her.

The witnesses who are condemning her are above reproach. Although she's fifteen, she'll be tried as an adult. Life in prison or death by lethal injection are in her future unless she can escape from prison, but then she must run for her life.

IV

Thanks to my granddaughter Eliana for
her help

VICKY'S ESCAPE

CHAPTER 1

"Mom! Mom!" There's no answer and I know what I'm going to find even before I get to the top of the stairs. Mom is sprawled across her bed, her long black hair covers her beautiful face. Unlike me, there's no doubt that Mom's Mexican. She was born in Juarez, and so was I. We moved to Albuquerque when I was four. Spanish is my first language and I guess I've got an accent.

Mom has passed out again tonight. Now there's no one to keep Dad from bugging me when he comes home from work. I'd like to blame Mom for what she's doing to us, but I think it's the only way she can stand to live with Dad. She's been really sad lately, and I'm worried about her. Not only is she dealing with Dad; Mom's an illegal and she's worried that she'll be deported.

Dad wasn't always such a tyrant. He had a head injury while serving in Afghanistan and it must have affected him, because since it happened he's been a different man. It's been two years since he got out of the VA hospital and he's still not getting any better. We're trying to be loyal and help him, but it's not working. Mom doesn't believe in divorce, and she's in a terrible situation.

I go into my room and lock the door. My new diary is in the top drawer of my night stand. It's a really good diary. It has a leather cover with a strap around it. I unlock it and start writing.

Gary Wheaton

Dear diary,

Mr. Nelson, is my guidance counselor. I told him that I was having trouble making friends and he advised me to get a diary and write in it every day, so here we go.

I'm a new student at Lincoln High and it's mandatory here for new kids to have a few sessions with the guidance counselor. I like Mr. Nelson. He and Mr. Jenkins, my English teacher, are my favorite teachers, but I like them all. Mr. Higgins, my gym teacher, is nice too, and I like Mrs. Young, the typing teacher. She likes me too, but it's probably only because I'm so much faster than everyone else. Physical things come easy for me. I wish math did.

The only kid in school that I'm friends with is Doreen. We met my first day here. It was her first day too. She's African-American. She considers herself to be black, but she's not much darker than me. I spend a lot of timer outdoors and I'm pretty tanned.

She's a little strange, but I like her. All the other girls here are snooty and all the boys look at me. The men look at me too, and sorry to say, when dad's drunk, sometimes he does too. Nothing has ever happened, but I'm afraid it might.

One night a guy from work came home with dad to watch the football game. Dad made me keep taking beers in to them and that guy really looked at me. Up and down. I felt self-conscious and uncomfortable.

Dad showed him his knife and told him about killing a guy with it in Afghanistan. He told the whole story in gruesome detail. Said he put his hand over the guy's mouth so he couldn't yell, then pulled the knife across his neck and sliced off a carotid artery. Just a few seconds and the guy dropped like a rock. He tells that story every time he gets drunk. He still keeps that knife really sharp. I know where it is, but I never touch it.

I hope this lock really works. I'd absolutely die if anyone read all this stuff and I'm just getting started.

I think Mr. Nelson and Mr. Jenkins are gay. I've seen them together after school.

Anyway, Mr. Nelson said I should start this diary by telling who I am. Or should it be whom. I don't know. So much for English class. Mr. Jenkins is kind of cute, too, but it's not going to work to have a crush on him anyway. I'm going to stick with who.

Well anyway, my name is Vicky, Victoria Avis Trent. I'm fifteen and a junior at Lincoln High taking the college course. That means that I'm taking math, which I hate. Not only am I not interested in quadratic equations; I can't think of anything that I could possibly ever use one for.

I look more like my dad than my mom, except that I'm only five four and weigh one hundred ten. Dad's a big guy, and really strong. I'm really strong too. I'll bet that I could beat most of the boys in my class at arm-wrestling.

I've got long blond hair and brown eyes. The guys think I'm cute, but here, it's more of a minus than a plus.

I'm an only child, and except for mom's mother who is old and has moved to Maine, I don't have any relatives besides Mom and Dad. I like to draw and paint. I paint a lot and I'm getting pretty good. I can sing and I won a talent contest back in Albuquerque. Also, I'm into running and gymnastics. I like to keep in shape.

Two weeks ago, Dad got transferred. People found out that he went berserk again even though he's been back from Afghanistan for two years. Everyone's scared of him. He works for a chain that services dishwashers in restaurants, and sells dishwashing chemicals. I'm sure they'd fire him if he wasn't so good at his job. He can fix anything.

Dad's Russian. I don't know why he was in Mexico. Anyway, I got born. I don't know if he and mom ever really got married.

We were renting a furnished house, so we just packed everything into the old Plymouth van and left in two days. We're used to moving. We just hopped onto I-40 and drove straight to North Carolina. We didn't pass GO or collect $200. We barely stopped to pee and eat a hot dog. I even got to drive some while Dad slept and Mom was sick. I'm not old enough, but I can drive okay. I've been driving some for a couple of years. No accidents so far.

In Albuquerque, I went to West Mesa School where all the kids were cool and I was happy.

Uh-oh. I just heard Dad pull into the driveway. That means he's going to fight with Mom if he can wake her up. If he can't, he'll bug me. I've saved most of my homework so that I'll have an excuse to be busy.

Goodbye. I'll try to write again tomorrow.

CHAPTER 2

When the door slams, I know that Dad is angrier than usual. He yells "Nora!" When she doesn't answer, he stomps up the stairs. I think I'm going to be okay tonight, but not Mom.

"Where were you? You didn't answer when I called at noon."

"I…"

"Get your lazy, drunken, worthless ass off that bed and get me some supper. You've got no idea how hard I work all day, and you can't even answer the phone and get me supper. I don't know why I put up with you. I should smack you up side the head."

"But..."

Sounds of a brief scuffle filter through my door, followed by thumping. He pushed Mom down the stairs. There are slow footsteps going to the kitchen. She isn't crying, so she can't be hurt very bad. The TV in their bedroom starts blatting, drowning out all the other noises.

I finish all my other homework and then try to figure out the math problems until Mom calls me for supper. No one talks while we eat.

After supper, I have to do the dishes because we don't have a dishwasher like normal people. We do still have Mom's pretty china with the yellow roses, though.

Mom and Dad have gone grocery shopping. I hope they don't fight in public again. I clean the kitchen, then hurry up to my room before they come home. I plug my ear buds in and work on math some more.

CHAPTER 3

I haven't been sleeping very well, and last night was no exception. Dad didn't say anything when I got in the car this morning. The day is about as normal as it gets around here. Going home at night is always stressful because I never know what my folks are going to do. At least Mom answers me when I go through the door. When I go upstairs, she's on the computer. She has been looking for an online job. I'm mad at her sometimes, but she's beautiful and I love her. She bought me this great pair of running shoes. She shouldn't have, because they were really expensive. Dad was mad about it, but she knows how much I like to run and she said that when she saw the "V" for Vicky on the sole, she knew they were meant for me. I tell her my day was okay, then go to my bedroom and lock the door.

Dear diary,

Today is Monday. I always wear tank tops, but Mondays and Wednesdays, I wear jeans instead of shorts. I do gymnastics on those days and change into gym clothes at school. I get plenty of exercise in gym, so I ride the bus home. Tuesdays and Thursdays I wear shorts because I run home. I wear my hair in a ponytail when I run. Fridays, I ride my bike because I do a weekly paper route. Saturday, I collect for the papers and go for a bike ride afterward. Sundays I go to church in the morning and run in the afternoon.

We haven't been here long, but I've already got a routine. I'm usually pretty organized. Girls don't normally do paper routes, but I needed some money and it fits with my exercise program.

Speaking of exercise, I had a good day at gym. I nailed a backflip on the beam four times and didn't get hurt once. No one even congratulated me except Mr. Higgins, the gym teacher. He told me once that I'm the best athlete he's had in years. Normally, though, he doesn't talk to me much. I wish he would. It would be nice to have someone appreciate me once in a while.

There's a guy in my history class who thinks he's a girl. I heard in gym class that his parents are fighting to have him use the girls' locker room. If the school board votes to allow it, I'll die. It's bad enough showering with those stuck-up girls.

Some of the boys are stuck-up too. Three of the seniors are football players and I heard in gym class that they're really good. Doreen says they think the world revolves around them, though. She says their folks are all high class. Jason Bentley's family has a fancy restaurant chain. Donny Gold's folks own Gold trucking. And Todd Richardson is the police chief's son. Doreen says they're all jerks. Donny's kind of cute, though.

I'd better say goodbye for now. Mom just went down stairs, so now the computer's free. I've got to print out some homework assignments before Dad gets home.

CHAPTER 4

Dear Diary,

Today is Tuesday. Mom was awake when I got home from school. That's good, but she still seemed pretty down. I wish there were something that I could do to make her feel better.

Not much new at school today. Still having trouble with math, but I think I actually learned something in class today. Maybe there's hope for me after all.

Doreen and I ate lunch together again today. No one else ever sits at our table. I don't think I'm ever going to be accepted at this school. Maybe I should join the band or the choir. I haven't played my flute for a while, but I'm sure it would come back pretty fast. I know I can still sing. I think it's too late to get on the basketball team.

Well, tomorrow is the big football game. We're playing the Charlotte Eagles, and they're supposed to be really tough. Doreen says she's going to the game so I guess I will too. I need to try to feel as if I belong at this school. I had better get started on my homework; I really need to spend some time on math. Goodbye for now. I'll try to write again tomorrow.

CHAPTER 5

It's late when I get home from school because of the football game. Mom is in her bedroom and I can hear her crying.

"Mom."

She doesn't answer.

"Mom."

Nothing. She's still crying. I knock on the door and then try to turn the knob, but it's locked. I give up and go to my room.

Dear Diary,

Today is Wednesday. Not much new today except the big football game. I'm not a football fan, but I have to admit that it was an exciting game. We played the Charlotte Eagles and until today they were undefeated. We were definitely the underdogs, but we beat them.

We have three seniors who are really good. They are the ones that Doreen says are stuck up: Jason Bentley, Donny Gold, and Todd Richardson. Todd, number twelve, practically won the game all by himself although he's smaller than most of the other players.

He made several great plays, but the last one was the most spectacular. He jumped to intercept a pass that everyone thought was way out of reach. He snagged it with one hand. He couldn't hang on to it, so he pulled it down to his chest, then sprinted through Eagle's defense to score the winning touchdown. It was a home game and the crowd went wild. They carried him off the field while the band played. He's definitely a hero. I don't know if he's stuck up or not, but I think he's great. He certainly is a super athlete. Even Doreen had to admit that he was pretty awesome. This is the first time that I've felt some loyalty to this school. It feels good, even though I still don't have any friends except Doreen.

I have to go do some homework. I'll try to write again tomorrow.

Dad still isn't home when it's time to go to bed. I check on mom, but her door is still locked, and she still doesn't answer when I call. At least she's not still crying.

CHAPTER 6

It's Thursday morning, and for once, Dad asks how school is going. It's been a long time since he has acted like he cared if I even existed, but by the way he asks, it almost seems as if he does. Maybe there's some hope after all.

"Okay," I tell him. "Today should be a routine day, no problems. Math is my worst subject, but I think I'm doing a little better."

"That's good. Look, I am going to be late again tonight; I'll get something to eat in town."

Not much of a conversation, but I'll take it. It's better than nothing.

At lunch, I sit at my usual table in the corner. Today, I'm alone. Doreen didn't come to school today. She told me that she misses two days every month.

Even though I went to the big game against Charlotte and cheered like mad, I don't really care much about football. That game was pretty exciting, but it's really not my thing. I know some guys like getting their brains rattled regardless of the consequences later on, but it doesn't make sense to me. Anyway, I've heard the three guys who come over and sit at my table described in terms that should be reserved for God. They're Lincoln's star football players, the ones who won the game. After last night, they're all heroes, and I have to admit that they were really super. I can't imagine why they'd be sitting at my table. The only one who ever sits here besides me is Doreen. I'm sitting at the far end of the table, next to the wall and these guys sit right across from me. They are the most popular kids in school, especially today, and I'm the least popular. It doesn't make sense.

"What do we have here?"

"I don't know, but she's a cute little thing."

"She may be cute, but I hear she's damned cold."

After last night, I kind of looked up to these guys, but those feelings are gone in a flash. They're keeping their voices low. No one else can hear them, but I can hear them well enough. I completely ignore them.

"She's not cold. She just needs someone to drag her to his bed caveman style. I think that's what they all really want."

"Sounds like a plan." It's mostly Todd who's doing the talking, but Jason has to get his two cents worth in too.

"I think I'll do it. Should be a lot of fun. I know where you live, too. Clarkey Brookey. What do you think, little quickie Vicky. A little quickie tricky would be fun, don't you think? I think it would, in fact, I think it will." He laughs and I can tell that he's proud of his little play on words.

That's Todd again. He's the superstar who made the winning touchdown. As far as I'm concerned, he's a superstar jerk. My lunch is only half eaten, but I jump up and push my chair back. It falls over with a crash. As I walk off, the whole lunchroom becomes silent and everyone looks at me. I turn back and stare at Todd.

"You're an idiot. You can think anything you want, but if you ever touch me, I'll bash your head in! And I know who you are. Your name is Toad."

A few snickers from the kids.

"My name is Todd." He has an angry scowl on his face, and he emphasizes 'Todd' as if I had mistaken it.

"Oh it's not Toad? Then it must be Turd."

A lot of snickers from the kids as I turn and stomp off.

CHAPTER 7

History is my last class. Mr. Nelson, the guidance counselor, meets me in the hall when it's over.

"Can you come to my office for a few minutes, Vicky? How long before the bus leaves?"

He has an uptight look on his face, like he doesn't want to tell me what's on his mind. I wonder if it's about the football players in the lunch room.

"Sure. I've got lots of time. I don't ride the bus Tuesdays and Thursdays."

He's tall and as we walk down the hall, he looks down at me.

"How do you get home?"

"I'm a runner. I run."

"Don't you live way out on the Clark Brook road?"

"It's not that far. It's only four and a half miles."

When we get to his office, Mr. Nelson sits behind his desk.

"Sit down." He points to a chair by the door. "You told me that you're having trouble making friends and I've checked with the other teachers."

He looks even more uncomfortable as he pauses.

"Prejudice is still alive even sat Lincoln. Rumor has it that your parents are volatile, and everyone seems to think that you're intimidating. You're very pretty and you're more mature physically than most of the other girls. The girls are jealous and the boys are afraid of you. One thing that might help would be to dress a little more…shall we say conservatively."

I don't say anything for a few seconds. I'm trying to decide how to respond. I like Mr. Nelson and I don't want him to think that I'm blowing him off.

I don't know why I'm considered physically mature. Runners don't have much fat, so we're usually short-changed where boobs are concerned. Not that I care. They just slow you down.

"Mr. Nelson, I'm a serious runner. I was contending for the state championship in New Mexico. This school doesn't even have a team. The most running I get to do is after school. When I run, I mean it. I'm completely exhausted when I get home. You can't run four and a half miles flat out in a skirt."

He looks almost shocked.

"I can see that we have more of a problem than I thought. Could you change after school?"

"How would I get my clothes home? You can't run with a backpack. Besides that, we aren't allowed in the locker rooms after class and I wouldn't go in there alone if we were."

"Let me think about it. There must be a solution. Have a good run."

I've been dismissed, and I'm relieved. He must not know about the lunchroom episode.

CHAPTER 8

After my little talk with Mr. Nelson, I start home. I'm all keyed up. I'll have to be careful to pace myself or I'll run out of gas before I get home.

I'm still running nearly flat out when I get to the strip of woods that's half a mile from our house. The back of a shiny blue SUV is flickering between leaves that are caught in the breeze. It's parked in the mouth of a short woods road. It's pretty. Dark blue. When I get opposite it, a big guy steps out of the bushes in front of me. It's Jason, one of the guys in the lunchroom. A football star. I instinctively turn to cross the road and out of the corner of my eye, I see someone behind me, back down the road to my left. Donny. I stop for half a second to catch my breath, and I'm grabbed from behind by a third person.

My captors don't say anything, they just drag me to the SUV which now has the rear door open. Even in my panic, I recognize that it's a Lincoln Navigator. I kick and yell and fight as best I can and I'm pretty tough, but after running four miles at my top speed, I'm also pretty tired.

Jason, the guy that jumped out in front of me has one arm under my shoulders while he has both my wrists in a vice-grip with his other huge hand. Todd, the guy that grabbed me from behind, has one arm locked under my butt while he gropes me with his free hand.

"Our little wetback is going to act tough. Grab her legs Donny."

I kick my legs, but he grabs them anyway.

As they stuff me into the SUV, Jason, the guy up

front has to release his hold on me. Todd, the guy in the middle pushes me inside while he pulls my shorts down. Because of all my thrashing, Donny has lost his grip on one of my legs. I yank my free knee up to keep Todd from pulling my shorts all the way off, then I arch my body and yell as I kick my free leg as hard as I can. That leg is super strong from all my running. It's had a few seconds to rest, and it's ready. My sneaker connects with something solid and I'm propelled into the big Navigator. I grab the door handle on the other side, but the door won't open. They must have the child proof lock on.

As Todd, the smallest of the three, bends inside and grabs my shorts again, I spot a liquor bottle under the back of the front seat. I grab it by the neck and pull my arm back to swing at him, but even in his compromised, bent-over position, Todd gets a hand on my weapon. Just like the football in the game last night. He's strong, but he doesn't know how strong *I* am, especially when I'm scared. As I twist the half full bottle out of his hand, the cap unscrews and I'm showered with vodka. He loses his balance and falls partially on top of me. He's still pulling my shorts off, but I'm sweaty and they bunch up around my ankles and don't slide off very easily. With all my strength, I smash his head with the bottle. It doesn't disintegrate like in the movies, but there's a solid, satisfying thud. He slides off me to the ground. Before I can get my shorts yanked up, my feet get caught in them and I almost fall back on Todd. As I claw my way between the front seats, I manage to get them pulled up. I fly out the driver's side door and hit the ground running.

When I'm two hundred feet up the road, I still can't

hear anyone chasing me. I'm tired and they might be able to keep up in a sprint, but there's no way they can catch me in the half-mile. If they chase me with the car, I'll run into the woods. I feel pretty safe. I stop to look back. Jason and Donny seem to be helping Todd into the Navigator. He's moving, but he looks drunk.

I still have the bottle in my hand. It's Smirnoff, the same kind Mom drinks. Then, I do a stupid thing. I'm all nerved up and completely exhausted. I tip the bottle up, hold my breath, and take a big swallow. It burns all the way down and cuts my breath off. I set the bottle in the bushes and wobble home.

CHAPTER 9

The front door is unlocked. That's different, but I've got more immediate things to worry about. I wonder how I'm going to keep Mom from finding out what has happened. I've got alcohol on my breath, and with all that vodka that got dumped on me, I smell like a brewery.

"Mom, I'm home."

At the top of the stairs, I see that she has the bathroom door closed. Luck is with me. Unless she comes out right now, I'm home free. I hurry past the bathroom and go to my room. I breathe a sigh of relief and lock the door. I'm safe, but we only have one bathroom. I'll have to wait for her to come out before I can get cleaned up.

Dear diary,

Well, today was an eventful day. I don't know where to begin. I'm pretty tired. I think I'll lay down on the bed and rest for a minute while I decide what to write.

Someone's banging on the door. I must have fallen asleep. Where's Mom? Why doesn't she see who it is? Maybe she's sick. I open my bedroom door. There's more banging coming from the front door downstairs.

"Coming!"

As I walk past the bathroom door, I step in water that's been running out from under it. It isn't water. It looks like blood.

"Mom!"

The bathroom door isn't locked. I slowly open it. I'm scared. As my eyes focus on mom lying on the cold, tile, floor, I feel vomit rising in my throat.

It looks as if Mom has a big cut on her neck. There's blood everywhere. I take dad's knife out of her hand. The handle is smoother than I thought it would be. I drop it in the sink.

"Mom!"

I get on my knees and hold her head, but she's already stiff. I'm crying as someone yanks my hands behind my back, pulls me to my feet, and puts handcuffs on my wrists.

"You're under arrest. You have the right to remain silent. Anything you say can and will be used against you in a court of…"

I feel my knees buckle.

CHAPTER 10

There are two policemen. As one of them drags me down the stairs, I can almost hear the other one talking on the radio. Cold calm voice.

"…1255 Clark Brook Road……from homicide….. Coroner's office…. stiff…meat-wagon...yes…Latino she's a mess."

That's my beautiful mom they're talking about. I hate them already.

I get shoved into the back of a vehicle for the second time today. This time, there's no fighting it.

"What are you doing with Mom? Did you call an ambulance?"

The cop that's driving doesn't say anything.

Although it's still daylight, I can see the flashing blue light reflecting from the cars we meet. At the police station, I'm taken directly to a small windowless room with a table and a couple of chairs. Just like on TV.

A cop comes in, takes my handcuffs off and then says the Miranda spiel again. Just to be sure I guess, or maybe they're recording it this time.

"Do you understand?"

"Yes."

He leaves and a few minutes later, comes back in with a camera. After making me stand against the wall, I have to hold up a plaque with my name on it while he takes my picture. Then, they leave me alone for what seems like an hour, before a different cop comes in.

"Hello. I'm detective Roberts. You've had a busy day."

This cop is tall and has a thin mean face. He pulls

the other chair out, turns it around backwards, and slowly sits.

"What are you talking about?" I'm still sobbing.

"First Todd Richardson, then your mother."

"You think I'd do something to hurt my mother? You must be crazy. Where's my dad?"

"I'm afraid it's not me who's crazy."

"Aren't I supposed to have a lawyer?"

From what I've seen on TV, now is a good time to ask that.

"I don't know what you need a lawyer for if you haven't done anything wrong."

I don't say anything. I don't like any of these guys and I'm not going to say anything until I've talked to a lawyer.

"All we're trying to do here is find out what happened tonight."

"Things will go a lot better for you if you talk to us."

When I don't say anything, Detective Roberts pushes his chair back under the table, and starts pacing. He sucks in his cheeks and that makes his face look even crueler. I can tell from his expression that he's done trying to be semi-pleasant.

"There are a hundred kids that heard you tell Todd that you were going to bash his head in and there are two kids that saw you do it."

I look at my watch.

"You know Todd is Chief Richardson's son, right?"

I don't answer, and he keeps on talking.

"Todd's the star quarterback on our football team and everyone loves him."

"Did you know that he's in the hospital with possible brain damage?"

"I can smell liquor on you from here. It's obvious that you've been drinking."

"I'd be willing to bet that your fingerprints are on that knife I saw in the bathroom lavatory."

"If you don't talk to us, we're going to have to throw the book at you."

"I don't care if you talk or not, but if you don't, we'll have to lock you up."

Detective Roberts turns and goes out the door.

CHAPTER 11

I'm sick about Mom. I've got her blood all over me, I'm tired and dirty, and I'm thirsty. After a long time, I lay my head on the table. I try to blank everything out and go to sleep, but the lights are too bright and besides, every time I close my eyes, I see Mom on the bathroom floor.

Eventually, the door opens and another cop comes in.

"Hi Vicky, I'm Jimmy."

Oh oh. The good cop. More TV training.

"You're a junior in high school, right?"

I stare at my hands.

"How'd you get to be a junior if you're only fifteen?"

I don't say anything.

"Look, I expect that you think we're out to get you, but I really would like to help you."

I put my head back down on the table.

"Come on Vicky. Talk to me."

When I don't move, Jimmy leaves.

It seems like forever before both detective Roberts and Jimmy come back into the room. Detective Roberts is the first to speak.

"We just found out that Todd has a serious brain injury. He's fighting for his life. You should have been trying to make a deal. If he dies, there won't be any deals."

"I think you had better talk to us before things get any worse," said Jimmy.

I don't know much about law, but I don't think cops

can make deals. I don't say anything.

"The whole town is mad as hell. You can't go around bashing the town hero in the head and get away with it. Especially when you're an outsider and people are already suspicious of you."

"Well, what do you say? Are you going to talk to us, or are we going to take you to jail?"

When I don't say anything, they both leave.

They leave me in the room alone for about an hour again, then the cop who drove me here walks in. I already know he doesn't talk and that suits me fine. He pulls my arms behind my back and handcuffs me again. As he pushes me down the hall, I tell him I'm thirsty. He leads me to a drinking fountain and pushes the button for me. I have a hard time getting a drink with my arms behind my back. I get water all over my face and the front of my tank-top.

My hands are still handcuffed behind my back when the seatbelt pulls me tight against the back seat. It hurts, but I don't give him the satisfaction of saying anything. When we get to the prison, they pat me down, but I'm not carrying anything. Then, they just put me in a cell. No supper, no shower, nothing. By now, all mom's blood has dried. It's itchy. There's another girl already in the cell. She's sitting on the bottom bunk rubbing her eyes. I know it must be well after midnight when I climb onto the top one and lay down. I think about mom, and cry for a long time.

CHAPTER 12

I wake to the sound of a horn. After about one second, the terrible reality hits me. My cellmate is already up. She looks cheerful and upbeat.

"Hi. My name's Marie."

"Hi. I'm Vicky." I try to act cheerful too, in spite of feeling rotten. "What's the routine here?"

"Right now, we go to breakfast, but first you need to take a shower. I can't believe they just put you in a cell with blood all over you. Usually they take your clothes when they book you in. Anyway, just follow me. We'll get you a shower and a clean uniform."

Marie is only fourteen. She's very friendly. By the time I'd known her for twenty minutes, she'd told me her life story. Her folks got sent back to Cuba, but she was born here, so she's a citizen. She couldn't make it on her own, so she started stealing. She knew that she'd eventually get caught, and sent to jail and they would take care of her. It was either that, or work as a prostitute.

The showers are big open places, and I'm dreading showering with a whole bunch of women. This morning, there's no one else in here. I'm alone. I'm already thinking that I may have to try to escape. I don't have any friends and Todd's a hero. If he dies, everyone will hate me. They probably do already. I guess his friends must not be saying that they were trying to rape me.

I take my sneakers off and stand under the shower with my clothes on.

"I'd like to wash my clothes."

Marie looks surprised, but she doesn't comment. I

lather up my clothes and rinse off.

"We normally shower in the afternoon after exercise." She says as she walks off.

I take my clothes off and finish showering and as I'm toweling off, Marie walks back in and hands me a clean uniform. The pants and shirt are stiff and orange. I put them on. They're too big, and they're ugly. Wouldn't do to wear these things if I can escape. I'd get caught in no time.

"I'd like to keep my clothes." I say as I wring them out.

Marie raises her eyebrows, but eventually she says, "I work in the laundry." She holds her hand out. She's speaking in Spanish and somehow that makes me feel better. It's like we're already friends. "I'll run them through the drier for you, but if they see them they'll take them away from you."

"Will you get in trouble?"

"No. I don't care anyway. I'm not going anywhere."

I'm sick about Mom, but I'm trying to stay positive. It looks as if Marie is going to be a good friend, and breakfast isn't half bad.

At ten o'clock, I have a visitor. Dad's eyes are red. He says they questioned him for half the night too.

"As soon as they determine the time of death, I'll be in the clear because I worked all day."

"I was probably in school."

"They won't set bail and I can't afford a lawyer, but they will have to provide one for you."

I tell dad the whole long story of what happened with the football players.

"This could be serious. I hear there's a good chance

the police chief's son might die."

The guard says our time is up already. Dad doesn't hug me or anything. He just leaves.

That afternoon, I get to meet my court-appointed lawyer. His name is Darrell Jones. He's overweight and sweaty in his black suit. His white shirt looks as if he's been wearing it for a week. Not that it's all that dirty, just wrinkled. Before we even talk, he has some papers for me to sign. He doesn't expect me to question anything. He just wants me to sign them. I don't cooperate.

"What's this one for?"

"It says you agree to waive the probable cause hearing. It's just a formality."

"What if I don't sign it?"

I think he has already decided that I'm not going to be easy. He starts explaining things.

"In North Carolina, serious cases go to superior court. There are three ways to get there. There's a probable cause hearing which is almost like a trial. The second way is for you to admit to probable cause. That happens when there's a plea bargain, a deal. In your case, they aren't going to be interested in a deal, especially if Todd Richardson dies. A nurse at the hospital told me that she'd give him a five percent chance of making it. The third way is when the case goes to the grand jury and they decide if there's enough evidence for a trial. There almost always is and that's what usually happens."

I've already decided that if Todd dies, I've only got one way to get out of here and that's to escape. After checking this place out a little, I don't see any way out. I think my best chance might be to try to escape from the courthouse, not from jail.

"Where are the trials and hearings held?"

"In the courthouse, but you don't have to go to the grand jury one."

"But I would have to go to the hearing?"

"Yes, but they almost never do it that way."

"Can I request it?"

"According to the law, yes, but I've never seen it happen."

"If I want to, will you request it?"

"Yes, but I don't know if it's a good idea to get the judge upset. If that boy dies, there's not a person in this town who wouldn't vote for at least life in prison. You've got to remember, you're new in town and a Latino. That shouldn't make any difference, but it will. Also, Todd Richardson is the police chief's son. He's a hero and everyone knows him and likes him."

"If everyone's mad already, is it going to make much difference if the judge is upset?"

"Probably not. I'm going to ask for a change of venue and he'll be upset about that anyway."

"What's that?"

"If there's a trial, and I'm pretty sure there will be, we don't want it to be here. Everyone here is already against you. We'll ask to have it moved, and the judge isn't going to like that."

For some reason, I already like this guy. Once he found out that I wasn't going to be hurried into anything, he changed his attitude. He doesn't treat me like an idiot. He explains things and he looks me in the eye when he talks to me.

"Okay, how about telling me what happened. Tell me everything that could be relevant. Don't leave anything out and don't sugarcoat anything. The prosecution is going to make everything sound as bad as possible and I want to hear it from you. I'm sticking my neck out here. Defending you is not going to win me any popularity points."

"Why are you doing it?"

"It's my job and besides, I have a soft spot in my heart for really pretty girls who are in trouble and you qualify."

CHAPTER 13

Marie helps me learn the ropes. She seems to know everything that's going on, even on the outside. She says everyone's upset about Todd. He's not getting better and the rumor is that he's dying. All the churches are holding prayer vigils for him.

Before long, I have a new routine. I've decided to be the most compliant prisoner this prison has ever had. I don't have much of a plan yet, but I know I'm going to have to gain the guards' trust. So far, I'm surprised by how nice they all are. I thought they'd be jerks like the cops were. I don't question anything they tell me. I just look at the floor and do what they ask. The only time I prove that I'm not half dead is during exercise time. When they see that I'm a serious runner they don't give me a hassle about my sneakers and they let me wear gym clothes.

I was beginning to think that my attorney had given up on me, but no, I eventually get another visit. When he comes in, he looks just…sad, and tired.

"Hello Vicky."

"Hello Mr. Jones."

"You may as well start calling me Darrell. We're going to be seeing a lot of each other for quite a while, I'm afraid. I've got some good news and some bad news."

He doesn't even give me a choice.

"The good news is that the coroner has determined a time of death for your mom. Ten AM. She called 911, but they had a hard time figuring out the message. She was crying and speaking partly Spanish. As near as they could tell, she was asking them to clean up the mess. She kept saying your name. I guess she didn't want you to find her. At first, they couldn't understand what the address was.

You were in school at ten am, and your dad was working. It was determined to be a suicide. I know that's hard to take, but at least, you're in the clear on that one.

The bad news is that Todd Richardson died last night from his brain injury. The charge against you has been changed to murder. Unlike most other states, in North Carolina anyone over the age of twelve is automatically tried as an adult for Class A felonies."

"What's a Class A felony?"

"Murder."

I just felt numb.

"Did they break down your door?"

"No. I guess mom must have left it unlocked"

"I'll check to make sure that they had a search warrant anyway."

"Will it really help our case if they didn't?"

"Probably not much, but it wouldn't hurt. When they questioned you, did they actually say they'd make a deal with you if you talked?"

"No, I don't think so, but they said Todd's condition was getting worse and that I should have been trying to make a deal. I should cooperate with them right away, because it would be harder if Todd didn't get better. They said that if Todd died, there wouldn't be any deals. They said it would go easier on me if I cooperated and that if I didn't cooperate, they'd have to take me to jail. They kept trying to get me to talk, but when they read my rights to me, they told me that anything I said would be used against me. I never said another word."

"Perfect. That's exactly what you should have done. Did they have a doctor examine you for bruises?"

"No."

"If they had, would they have found any?"

"No."

"How much vodka did you drink?"

"One swallow."

"Do you normally drink?"

"No."

"Did you humiliate Todd in the lunchroom?"

"Yes, or at least, I certainly tried to."

Darrell questions me for a long time. I try to answer his questions truthfully, but I can tell that he's discouraged.

When I get back to the cell, Marie confronts me immediately

"What happened?"

I've already told her all about hitting Todd. I like her and trust her.

"Well, Todd died. Now they've charged me with murder."

"Oh no."

I tell her everything including Darrell's statement that I'd be tried as an adult because I'm over twelve years old and the impression I got that Darrell seemed discouraged with our case.

"I don't know what to do. I like Darrell and he believes me, but they've got witnesses that are willing to lie about what happened. I think my only hope is to get out of here."

Marie doesn't say anything. I thought she might try to talk me out of trying to escape, but she doesn't. I already think I know what a terrible life running from the law would be, but I also know that it would be better than no life at all.

CHAPTER 14

Darrell was right. The judge is in a snit about the probable cause hearing thing. He sort of threatened him, but Darrell held his ground. Bless his heart. He hasn't hit him with the change of venue yet, but Darrell says he should be expecting it because the whole town's mad at me. I wouldn't be able to get a fair trial here.

The hearing is scheduled for ten-thirty next Thursday. Darrell doesn't think it will last very long. It's just a gut feeling, or intuition, or something, but I'm convinced that the hearing at the courthouse is probably going to be my only shot at getting out. I'm trying to come up with a plan and I'm starting to get some ideas. I trust Marie now and I need her help. I tell her what I'm going to try to do.

I carry out the first part of my sketchy plan early Wednesday morning. Marie hides my extra clothes in her bed, then I vomit all over myself in my bed. It's messy, but it accomplishes three things. Practice throwing up, clean pajamas, and establishing that I'm sort of sick. Marie yells for a guard, then gets clean pajamas and bedding from the laundry while I shower.

I mope around all day and at exercise, I don't do enough to get sweaty. I think my gym top might be less noticeable than the tank-top I was wearing when they arrested me so I leave it on and put my orange top on over it.

My escape uniform will be my regular running shoes, my shorts, the ones that Todd was pulling off me, and the prison gym top that I'm hiding under my orange shirt. If it doesn't look too bulky under my orange uniform, I'll wear my pajama top too.

I'm nervous when we have inspection that night. Under my pajamas, I'm wearing my gym top and my shorts. I try to act sick, but not sick enough to see the doctor.

CHAPTER 15

I'm so scared and excited that I don't sleep very well. This is probably my only chance. My whole life is riding on what I do for the next few hours. I get up early and pull my orange uniform on over my escape attire. I ask Marie what she thinks.

"I don't think you look too bulky even with the pajama top and gym top on."

"I hope not. If they notice, I'm sunk."

I hug Marie and tell her I'll try to write. After thinking about it, though, writing to her might help them track me down.

"Actually, I might not be able to write for a while, but I won't forget you and I'll try to contact you somehow."

I haven't known Marie very long, but I know that I'm going to miss her. I have to be careful not to get too emotional when we go to breakfast. I try to give the impression that I'm just picking at my food, but this might be my last meal for a while, and I'm going to throw some of it up. I temporarily give up on acting sick, and eat everything on my tray. Marie gives me some of her French toast too. We have to be careful that someone doesn't see us. There's orange juice which I drink along with a lot of water.

A guard comes for me at nine o'clock. Two police officers that I haven't seen before are waiting to take me to the courthouse. It's a man and a woman. I'm happy to note that although the man is huge, the woman is not much bigger than me. She's a Latino too. They handcuff me with my hands in front. I don't look at them. I just try to act sick as they lead me to their cruiser.

We get to the courthouse a little early and I study

the structure carefully as we walk inside. It's an old building, stone exterior with narrow ledges running under the windows. Four stories. I stumble up the outside stairs to the entrance with a cop on either side. I've been hoping that the courtroom would be on the first or second floor, but when we get into the old elevator, the lady cop pushes the button with a four on it. It even smells old in here. The ancient thing's really slow. It creaks and groans, but we finally get to exit it and walk down a long corridor. Even though it's an old building, it has nice polished hardwood floors.

As we near the courtroom, I speak for the first time.

"I don't feel very well. I need to use the ladies' room."

"You're just nervous."

"I've got to use the ladies' room."

The lady cop makes a face as she pushes on the big old dark wooden door beside the one marked 'courtroom.' The heavy door looks as if it belongs in an old castle or maybe a dungeon. She leads me into the little restroom. Her partner waits in the hall.

As the door swings outward to close, I estimate how large the gap under it is. It's a one person restroom. Just a lavatory and a commode. No privacy stall. There is, however, a lock on the heavy old oak door which also has an automatic closer. There's an old steam radiator under the little window on the outside wall.

I hold out my hands, switching my focus back to the floor. She sighs as she takes my cuffs off. I check how thick the toilet seat is and determine that the tank cover looks removable and sturdy. I find it a little difficult to pee with someone watching me, but I drank a lot of water at breakfast time, and finally, I succeed. I check out the window while I wash my hands and face. It has a latch but it's probably been crippled. The glass is imbedded with, what appears to be chicken wire. Not really very sturdy. Maybe I can break it out.

After I've checked out the restroom all I'm going to be able to without the lady cop becoming suspicious, I get some paper towels from the dispenser and dry my hands and face. Then the little cop puts my cuffs back on and she and her partner lead me into the courtroom. It's a big old dark room with a lot of chairs in it. Darrell is already here.

"How are you?" He asks automatically.

"I feel sick," I say loudly enough for the cops standing behind me to hear.

CHAPTER 16

We all stand as the judge walks in. He's scowling. Darrell said he was going to be upset because he didn't want to have a hearing. Too bad.

"This is not a trial. We're just going to determine if there's probable cause to have a trial. Does anyone have information that's pertinent to that question?"

"I Do."

A man whom I assume is the prosecuting attorney stands up.

The judge waves his arm and says, "Go ahead, we're going to be informal here."

"Well I don't think there's any question that the suspect killed Todd Richardson. He and two friends stopped to help this girl." he pointed at me. "because they thought she was in trouble. It turns out she was drunk and she hit…"

"Objection."

"This isn't court, but what is your objection?"

"What makes Mr. Jacobs think my client was drunk?"

"She reeked of alcohol."

"Can you get drunk from an external application of alcohol now? My client got drenched with alcohol while fighting to keep Mr. Richardson from pulling her pants off. They were in the process of raping her."

"That's ridiculous."

"Was the defendant given a blood alcohol test?" the judge asks.

"No, your honor, she wasn't. It seemed obvious, and besides, they weren't fighting with her. The only fighting that was done was when she hit Todd."

"They weren't fighting?"

"No. You expect us to believe that if they had been fighting, this little girl could have fought off three big football players and killed one of them without getting so much as a scratch?"

I lay my head on the table.

"Objection."

"Now what?"

"I haven't read the doctors report. Was there one, or is Mr. Jacobs an expert in that field also?"

I hide what I'm doing with my arm as I stick my fingers down my throat and barf all over the table. Some gets on my orange top, but I don't care. I'm going to have to ditch it anyway. I slowly get up.

"I'm sick."

The female cop grabs my arm and leads me back to the little bathroom. She has a disgusted look on her face as I drag my feet and act as if I'm trying to keep from vomiting again. Once inside the restroom, she lets the door close automatically. I stagger, then wildly grab for her to keep from falling. I fall anyway, backwards onto the hard tile floor. The only thing my hand closes on is the cord to her microphone. It goes to the floor with me, killing her radio. What sounds like my head hitting the floor, is actually my shoulder. If there was anything that I've learned in gymnastics, it's how to fall.

I don't move except for my eye lids fluttering and drool running out of the side of my mouth. Blood would be nice, but my plan doesn't call for it. I couldn't think of a way to get some that didn't involve pain.

The cop bends down and removes my cuffs.

"Victoria! Victoria!"

When I don't respond, she rushes out the door.

"Call an ambulance!" she screams.

I jump up, override the automatic door closer by pushing the door closed; then I quietly lock it. It takes me three tries to yank the toilet seat off. I'm worried about how long it's taking me as I wedge it under the door and hammer it tight with the toilet tank cover. That should jam the door. They'll never be able to open it without breaking something.

After climbing onto the radiator, I try to unlock the window. Doesn't work. The lock on the window has been permanently jammed. I jump down off the radiator and grab the flush tank cover again. While I repeatedly ram it against the window, glass flies everywhere. Finally, the whole sash collapses and falls out. It takes a long time to hit the parking lot, reminding me of just how high I am.

Someone is banging on the door as I climb through the opening. The ledge running around the building is narrower than it looked from the ground and from four stories up, the parking lot is a long way down. The corner is only twelve feet away, but it seems really far. I take a deep breath and try to pretend that the skinny ledge is a balance beam. I can't get my balance, though. I'm already against the wall. The only direction I can move to get my balance is toward the parking lot.

The banging on the door gets much louder as I stand on the ledge and flatten my back against the bricks. My toes stick out over the edge. I slide the side of my face along the wall to keep my center of gravity as close to the building as possible. I can't move one foot past the other. I have to inch one over, then move the other one over to it. It's taking too long, but I can't hurry. I'm only four feet from the corner when I almost fall. There's a depression in the ledge where they used a brick that is thinner. I can't turn my head, so I didn't see it.

The ledge doesn't wrap around the corner, but decorative blocks form the angle where the walls join. They're staggered, providing handholds. As I slowly work my way around, there's a big crash inside. They've broken the door.

Just around the corner is a drainpipe that's hooked to the gutter above me. I might be able to climb down it in time to get away if I hurry. As I grab it and put my weight on it, it pulls out of the gutter above me and drops about two feet. I think my heart has stopped as I dangle over the edge. When my brain starts working again, I feel a sharp pain in my left hand. My heart finally resumes beating and I climb back onto the ledge. I check out the drainpipe and my hand. The drainpipe's a lost cause. The bracket that I cut my hand on pulled out of the bricks when I swung back to the ledge. The drainpipe would never support me now. My hand isn't hurt very badly, but it *is* bleeding. Some blood has already run down the drainpipe. I quickly squeeze as much as I can into the palm of my right hand and throw it onto the driveway below. A perfect trail for them to follow.

I'd like to keep going to the next corner, maybe there's a better drainpipe there, but I don't think I've got time. The ledge is so narrow that I might not make it anyway. I hope they're done sticking their heads out of the broken window as I move back around the corner into view and climb up the offset blocks as fast as I can. Around the edge of the flat roof, is a sheet-metal trim or something that forms the gutter. It sticks out about a foot. I climb up to it and put my arm up over it trying to find a handhold. Nothing, just smooth metal. To climb up more, I have to pull out away from the wall. If I can't reach something to hold onto, I might not be able to climb back down. Although I've been willing myself not to look down, I can't help it. The parking lot is even farther down than when I was on the ledge. I've already leaned out too far. If there isn't anything up there to grab, I'm going to fall, four stories. My throat is dry and the skin on the back of my neck feels tight.

There's no turning back now. I pull myself up even farther. Gravity is starting to pull me away from the building when my right hand closes on the sharp inside edge of the sheet-metal. I didn't fall, but I can't hang here for long. Even if I cut my hand badly, I've got to pull myself up enough to get my other arm over the top. To do that I have to pull myself out away from the corner even more and up the metal gutter that encloses the perimeter of the roof. When I do, my feet lose traction. As the fingers of my left hand finally curl around the sharp metal edge of the gutter, my body swings free, only supported by my aching fingers. Pulling myself up as far as I can I swing a leg over the gutter. I never would have been able to pull myself onto the roof without my gymnastic training. I didn't get much blood on the metal, but I carefully wipe it all off. I try to spit on it to wash it off, but I don't have any spit. When I stop shaking, I look around. I'm out of sight, temporarily at least.

Before Dad went to Afghanistan, we rented a cabin on a remote lake. That was the best week of my life. Dad was fun back then. Mom was small like me. She used to say that he was her big strong man. He was too. He would say that I was his little strong girl.

Anyway, there was an outhouse at the lake, just like

the one in the middle of this roof. This one is locked, though, and probably doesn't have a seat with a hole in it. I expect that someone will be coming through that door looking for me eventually. There's also a big curved vent of some kind and a huge fan. My current plan is to find a place to hide until dark, but before I do I have to find a way down. I'd never be able to get down the way I came up. I have to find another way down now, and I may not have much time.

I don't dare to get too close to the edge of the roof for fear that someone on the ground will be able to see me. I'm in a big hurry as I check all the way around the roof for escape possibilities, but I manage to find two. There's an antenna up here and the wire is running down the side of the building. It's pretty small, but it might help me get down onto the ledge. I isn't very close to a corner, though and I don't think I could walk very far on that ledge in the dark. The other possibility is a big live oak tree. The top of it is about one floor down and it's about ten feet away from the building. I might be able to jump into the top of it. I know I can jump that far, but hanging on once I land might be a problem, especially in the dark. On the next street over, there's a streetlight that I can line up with if it comes on. Even if I get into the tree without killing myself, though, I'd still have to climb down and I can't see what the bottom of it looks like. It's not a very good option, but I think it's the best one.

The big vent seems like a good place to hide. It might go all the way to the basement, though. I peel a piece of loose asphalt from around its base and drop it into the opening then listen. One-thousand one, one-thousand two, clunk. Sixteen feet the first second and thirty-two feet per second per second...About forty-eight feet. Maybe math and physics are good for something after all. I guess I won't jump in there.

The big fan is a possibility. It has a shroud around it and a louvered cover. It doesn't look as if I could fit between the louvers, but I'm desperate and when I try, I discover that they are flexible. By pulling them apart, there's room for me to squeeze between them and lie on the radiator between the fan blades. Looks perfect, but what if the fan starts? The wire from the fan motor runs to the frame where there's a metal box with a shutoff lever on the side. Our air-conditioner in Albuquerque had a smaller one, but it looked similar. It had cylindrical fuses in it. I pull the lever down to kill power, then open the cover and pull the three fuses out. I drop them straight down into the big curved vent, being careful not to let them clunk against the side of the big duct. I close the cover on the box and then climb into the fan. It's uncomfortable and hot in here and it's going to be a long time before it gets dark. I've got to tough it out, though. If I get caught I'm going to be a lot more uncomfortable. Before long I realize that if the air conditioner comes on, I'm going to be in trouble. The fan won't come on, but the radiator that I'm lying on is going to get hot. The sun is high and it's already starting to get warm. There's a good chance that the air conditioner will come on before the afternoon is over. I think I remember seeing some valves on the outside of the fan enclosure. I hurriedly start to climb out of the fan enclosure. Uh-oh. I hear the outhouse door opening.

CHAPTER 17

I quickly get back into the fan enclosure. I'm in the same position I was in before I started to get out. The shroud has some tiny holes in it and I've positioned myself so that I can see out through one of them. Two police officers hurry across the roof to the corner that I climbed up over and examine the metal gutter. I don't know if they saw something suspicious or not, but one of them runs around the perimeter of the roof while the other one examines the big vent. The louvers in the fan enclosure don't look big enough for anyone to go through them, so they don't even look at it. They are only on the roof for a couple of minutes before they hurry back to the door. I can hear them talking.

"Did you see anything?"

"Nope. How about you?"

"Nothing. She must have gone down the drainpipe. I don't think anyone could climb up here anyway. She never could have gotten over that gutter. I certainly wouldn't want to try it and I'm a lot taller than she is."

"Yeah, if she had tried that we'd have found her splatted on the parking lot."

"You know if we don't find her pretty soon, the FBI will find her and steal all the glory."

"Always do."

As soon as the door in the outhouse closes, I climb out of the fan enclosure. The valves that I remembered seeing aren't manual valves. They're electrically operated and the wires hooked to them don't go to the fuse box that I sabotaged. I read the little metal tag on the one that's most accessible. "240 V   APPLY

POWER TO OPEN." There are three wires. A black, a white, and a green. When Dad worked on electrical things, he said the black is usually hot. It's the one that usually makes things work. The green is ground. I don't have any tools, so I grab the plastic insulation on the black wire and twist it back and forth. It's not breaking off very fast. The valve makes a heavy 'click,' and the pipe that it's hooked to starts getting hot. If I can't break the wire off, the radiator is going to get hot and I won't be able to lie on it. Frantically, I yank on the wire. It pulls out of the clip that's hooked to the end of it and when it hits the body of the valve, sparks fly. In a few minutes, the pipe cools down and I climb back into the fan enclosure.

I've finally got time to think about Mom and cry. I wonder if there was anything I could have done to make her feel better. I certainly wasn't a very good daughter. I was so involved with my own problems that I didn't have much time for her. I was almost happy when dad picked on her because that meant that he'd leave me alone. I was pretty selfish and now it's too late.

I've got to stop thinking those negative thoughts. I need to make some more plans, but I don't know how I can because I don't know what's going to happen. I've got to get rid of these orange clothes, but not before I climb down the tree. The thick rough cloth might keep me from getting all scratched up.

I wonder what Dad will do now. Maybe he'll finally get some psychiatric help. He needs it and the VA will help.

If I had it to do over, would I hit Todd so hard? Probably. I was scared out of my mind. He was a fantastic football player, and everyone thought he was a real hero, but he wasn't a very nice person. I'm sorry that he died though.

How am I going to make it on the outside? What am I going to eat? It's going to be hard to survive without getting caught. They'll put my picture in the paper and everyone will recognize me. I think my best bet is to get out of this area.

CHAPTER 18

I have a long wait, but it finally starts to get dark. The sound of traffic on the streets below changes. Now it's not cars rushing around, it's just someone occasionally driving past. I think they've decided that I'm not such a dangerous fugitive that I'm worth missing supper over.

That theory holds until several more cars pull into the parking lot. I vacate my hiding place and sneak a look over the edge. The guys getting out of the cars have shirts marked FBI. I think I'm going to have to stay put for a while longer.

It's going to take this new crowd a while to get organized, so I take advantage of the time by walking around and stretching out the kinks. From up here, I can see the layout of the city. Residential behind the courthouse, business to the front. What looks like a truck stop is off to the left. That's tempting. Get out of Dodge quick. I don't think so. I'm sure they'll be watching it for days.

After a while, all the new guys in the parking lot gather around one person. Must be the boss. I go to the edge of the roof at the back and check out my escape tree again. It doesn't look very inviting in the dark, but the streetlight on the next block over is shining on the leaves. I've already decided that it's going to have to be my avenue of escape and since the FBI will probably search the roof, I'm going to have to do it before too long. I could hide and wait for the FBI to leave. That would give me more time and getting down with less pressure would be better. "You're just putting it off because you're afraid to jump into that tree." I tell myself under my breath.

I go back to see what the FBI guys are doing. A white van pulls into the parking lot. As it passes a pole with some of the parking lot lights on it, I can read the writing on the side. "Dr. Cool Air Conditioner Expert." Uh-oh. That guy is here to fix the stuff I've disabled. I've got to get off this roof, now, before he comes up here. When I checked it out, the tree looked thick enough to hide in, especially in the dark. "Okay, you've put it off long enough. Now do it. If you wait any longer, you'll just get more nervous."

While the FBI guys are all huddled around out front, and Dr. Cool isn't up here yet, I get a running start and while trying not to leave scuff marks with my sneakers, I sprint to the back of the courthouse. I'm really scared as I jump into the top of the big old live oak. For some reason, I don't die. I'm shook up a little, but my landing is softer and quieter than I thought it would be. The branches in the top of the tree are small and flexible. They slowed me down so that I didn't jump right through them onto the street below, but they didn't hurt me either. I can't believe how lucky I am. I was hoping to not get killed, and I didn't even get hurt.

I quietly climb down into the thickest part of the tree and find a branch to sit on. Not exactly comfortable, but at least I'm not all scratched and bleeding, and I'm not all scrunched up like I was in the fan.

I shield my watch so that its dim light won't show and keep track of the time. By one o'clock, everything's quiet. All the lights are out in the courthouse, and I don't hear Dr. Cool moving around on the roof anymore. I wait until just after two and then start down the tree.

When I get to the lowest branches, I know I'm still a long way from the ground. I can't tell exactly how far because of the shadow from the house across the street. The whole bottom half of the tree is dark. I slide off the lowest limb in complete darkness and wrap my legs around the trunk. I'm glad I've still got the orange prison uniform on. The heavy cloth keeps my arms and legs from getting all scratched up. I can barely get my arms around the trunk enough to hang onto the rough bark and I know the bottom of the trunk will be bigger. As I get lower, the trunk gets so big that I can no longer reach half way around. I'm having trouble hanging on. I have to find handholds in the bark. It's slow work, but I'm making progress. Then, what I've been fearing happens. I have no idea how high I am when the piece of bark that the fingers of my right hand are clinging to breaks and I fall. The panic only lasts for seven microseconds, because I only fall two feet. Not only am I safely on the ground; there's no one waiting with handcuffs. What a relief.

CHAPTER 19

There are several businesses on the first floor of the old courthouse, and there's a dumpster out back for their trash. I'm sure that it will be searched because the FBI will go to great lengths to uncover clues. I find a dead branch and use it to stuff my orange uniform far underneath the dumpster. I hope it will be several days before the trash is picked up and they find my suit.

Three AM is not a good time to be wandering around the city. I need a place to hunker down for the rest of the night and I decide to try a residential street. If the police are patrolling, I'll hear the cruiser in time to hide. I'm dying of thirst and the first house I come to has an outside spigot with a hose attached. I turn the water on and can't wait for the water to clear out of the hose. The water tastes yucky, but it's wet. I continue on down the street, looking for a house with a "for sale" sign and a lawn that needs mowing.

A garage door across the street unexpectedly opens and a car quickly backs out. I'm caught in the open. As I run for a rosebush to hide behind, the car swings around and its lights find me. It slows down when it gets to the rosebush, then speeds off. In two minutes, I hear a siren, but I'm almost a half-mile away.

So much for the residential plan. They might check house to house for all I know. It's obvious that they badly want to catch the fiend who killed the star quarterback, who was also their boss's son. I sneak between houses and head over to the truck stop.

I was right. There's a cruiser at each end of the parking lot and one pulled up in front of the restaurant. I watch for a few minutes and whenever a truck pulls in, the police stop it and do a search. I don't know why they're searching the ones coming into the truck stop, but I guess they aren't taking any chances. They're covering all the bases. There are some trucks backed up to the fence around the left side of the parking lot that don't seem to be guarded. Apparently they've already been searched and the police don't think anyone can get past them to hitch a ride. I sneak through the bushes, hoping not to step on a snake and come out behind the fence.

One of the trucks has canvas across the back instead of doors. The canvas is laced on both sides, but not on the top or bottom. The fence is about as high as the top of the box. It has a tight mesh and a strip of barbed wire on top. It's going to be hard to climb even for a gymnast. That's why the cops aren't worried. It's hard on the fingers and the barbed wire is a challenge. I manage to climb to the top of it and by laying my shirt on it, avoid getting ripped up by the barbed wire. From there, it's an easy jump onto the top of the box. I squeeze under the canvas and drop to the floor inside the trailer.

The parking lot was lit up like noontime, but where the trucks are parked, it's darker. Better for the drivers to sleep, I guess. Inside the truck body it's completely dark and I've got no idea what's in here. I wait until my eyes are as acclimated to the dark as they are going to get, then I push the button on my watch. It illuminates an area of bare floor. That's good enough for me. I haven't had any real sleep for a long time, and it's been a stressful day. I lay down and go to sleep, hoping that I won't wake up in North Carolina.

CHAPTER 20

It seems as if I couldn't have been asleep for more than five minutes when I hear the air brakes release and the truck starts moving. Good, we're on our way. I try to go back to sleep, but we keep going around corners and hitting potholes. When we get on the highway it should be better.

There's a skylight in the roof and when we go under a streetlight, it's momentarily light inside the box. I can see that the truck is empty except for a stack of furniture pads. It's a good thing I've got good balance because it's tricky getting over to them without falling down. I sit on the pads and hang onto a ring that's recessed into the side of the box for support.

It must be a traffic light that we're stopped for now. It could be a police check. If it is, I'm caught and I'll never get another chance to escape. No sense worrying about it though, there's nothing that I can do about it. We're stopped right under a streetlight. I turn to look around and my leg hits something. Two boxes are buried in the pile of pads. I have just enough time to check their contents before we move again, cutting off the light. I'm no expert, but I'd guess the hidden boxes contain marijuana.

After fifteen minutes, we still haven't gotten to the highway. Instead, we slow down and then stop. We back up, stop, I hear the brakes, and then the engine shuts down. I hope that before long it will start back up and we'll go to California and pick up a load of oranges. I could sure use an orange right now. Instead, the lacing on one side of the canvas is being undone and a light comes on inside the box. I hide behind the pile of pads and peek over the top. A big guy with a belly moves the canvas aside, climbs up into the box and walks up toward me. He doesn't see me until he gets almost to the pads.

"Hey! You're the girl they were looking for at the truck stop. I saw your picture. You sure don't look like a Latino."

He's blocking the way out and with his long arms, I know I'll never be able to get past him. I try anyway. I almost get away too, but when I climb over the stack of pads, he grabs my wrist.

"Where do you think you're going?"

He looks just like a regular guy. He could be someone's father. He may be paunchy, but he's very strong. He gets a better hold on my arm, and I think he could snap it just by squeezing. I know that I can't fight him.

"Okay you've got me. Now what?"

"What do you mean, now what? I'm going to take you to the police station. Did you know there's a reward for you?"

"No, I didn't. You know that I killed a football player, right? Do you really think you can get me down out of this box without getting hurt?"

"Oh I think I probably can."

My heart is beating pretty fast, but I try not to let him see how scared I am.

"Let's put it another way. Would it make any difference if I could convince you that it wasn't my fault?"

"Probably not, but I've got lots of time. Tell me what happened."

"If I stand over here, can you grab my hand or

something? My arm's turning black."

He listens without interrupting while I tell him the whole story.

"That's not what they said on TV."

"They always get it wrong. I did hit him, but I didn't intend to kill him. He was raping me. What could I do?"

"I don't know. I guess it's your word against theirs. The court should decide it."

"Oh sure. I'm apt to get a fair trial in this town. They already hate me. Let's put it another way. I think it's a matter of trust."

"How's that?"

"If I can trust you not to call the police, you can trust me not to tell them about these boxes, even if I get caught. If you get me something to eat, that is."

"I can see that we've got a problem."

"Not unless you make it one. You do have to either trust me or kill me and I don't think you could kill me."

He lets go of my hand.

"What do you want to eat?"

CHAPTER 21

He picks up the two boxes and leaves the truck where it's parked with a bunch of other trucks at a terminal building. I don't even know his name, but he takes me to Burger King in his car and buys me two Whoppers, fries, and a shake, plus an extra bottle of water. He gets a breakfast sandwich and coffee for himself.

"Actually, I do believe you. What can I do for you now?"

"Take me to a park or someplace where I can run. If we could, I'd like to stop and get a cap and some cheap sunglasses. If they're using my picture, I've got to be careful."

"I can do better than that. There are some sunglasses in the glove compartment and I think there's a hat on the back seat."

We drive through an old-looking section of town. Close packed houses and convenience stores with bars over the windows. He lets me off at a wooded area with trails where even at this early hour, people are running. When he shakes my hand goodbye, he pushes a twenty dollar bill into my palm.

"Good luck."

"Thank you, thank you."

He drives off and I stand there thinking how lucky I am. Since I don't have any pockets, I stuff the bill into my sneaker. As I mess with the cap's adjustable band, I notice the name. Gold Trucking.

I walk up the trail for a few minutes to limber up before I stop and take the prison pajama top off. After hiding it and my water in the bushes, I stretch a little, then I run. Everyone seems to be going the same direction, and most of the people I pass are just jogging. I'm running fast and the few that I meet don't really have time to get a good look at me. It feels good to be free as I run on the beautiful trail. I wear down quickly, though. I just ate, and it's been a long time since I've had any real sleep. When the sun starts warming things up I go back, pick up the shirt and have a drink of my water. A little way off the trail, I find a secluded grassy spot in the woods and walk around to check for snakes and other creepy-crawlies. It's dry and it looks okay, so I put on my shirt, crawl into the shade of a little pine tree, and fall asleep.

CHAPTER 22

I hear someone or something coming. They're not moving at a steady pace. Sounds like they might be sneaking along trying not to step on dry twigs. I don't know if I should jump up and run, or stay put. I think I'm pretty well hidden and he or it, is wandering around, not coming directly toward me. I lie perfectly still, not even opening my eyes. Maybe they will go away.

It's making a different sound. Moving the leaves. I'll bet it's a wild boar. It doesn't really sound like a person who's trying to catch me. More like a wild boar who doesn't know that I'm here. I could run, but I think they're really fast. Probably territorial too. I wonder if this tree that I'm lying under is big enough to climb.

Suddenly whatever I'm hearing is much closer. Not big enough for a wild boar. I'll bet it's a copperhead. I know they have a lot of them here. Now I don't dare to move. I can almost feel that thing biting me, and it's going to if I so much as twitch.

It's right by my head. I can hear it slithering by my ear. It's doing something above my head. It has raised up to strike me in the face. My eyes fly open although I didn't tell them to. I'm staring into the shiny black eyes of a squirrel who's perched on a limb right above my face.

When I've calmed down a little from my unfounded fright, I look at him closely. He's not at all afraid of me although he's less than two feet above my face. His little whiskers twitch inquisitively as he watches me. If I move, he'll be gone. He's like a sprinter waiting for the starting pistol. Bright sunlit pine needles surround him.

He's beautiful. Finally I have to move and he disappears to scold me from the top of the little tree.

I check my watch. Quarter past two. What am I going to do now? It's not going to work to try to leave the area. If they're watching truck stops, they'll definitely be watching bus terminals, airports, any transportation that could get me out of North Carolina. Looks like I'm going to be stuck here for a while. I need to find a place to spend the night.

I've been wearing my hair in a ponytail since I got arrested, but I pull off the elastic and stretch it around my wrist. My hair falls down in all directions. I put the hat on and my hair covers everything except my face. The sunglasses do a pretty good job of that. I don't think people will recognize me.

There are still a few people jogging on the trails. I jog too, slowly and in the direction of downtown. The trail I'm on comes out in an area that has houses and stores. I slow down and walk along the sidewalk. A variety store that I pass has a selection of newspapers in front. They all have my picture. If I stop, someone might notice me. I only have time to read a few of the headlines:

> Killer still on the loose.
> Reward now at $100,000.
> Dogs track Todd's killer to truck-stop.

And of course the tabloids:

> Her mind is controlled by aliens.
> Fear of possessed girl grips city.

Wow! They've even got dogs looking for me. A hundred-thousand dollars is a lot of money. If that truck driver tells them where he took me, dogs could track me down in no time. I've got to do something to throw them off my trail.

I start slowly jogging again. When I see a taxi, I wave him down. Even a short taxi ride would throw the dogs off.

"103 Elm Street," I tell him.

I think almost all towns have an Elm Street. I assume this one does too. When we stop for a red light, the foreign-looking driver stares at me in the mirror and I know he recognizes me. I can almost see one-hundred-thousand dollars registering in his eyeballs. He yells at me, but I'm out the door before the light turns green. I run between two houses and come out on the next street over. I know the police will be here in a matter of minutes.

CHAPTER 23

Now I'm in a panic. I've got to get out of here and not leave a trail that dogs can follow. Down at the end of this street is a bus stop and people are getting on. Wait for me I pray, as I sprint down the street still clutching my water bottle. This could solve my problem if the bus driver doesn't recognize me.

I'm halfway to the bus when the last person gets on. I put on another burst of speed and wave my arms, but I see black smoke spew from its exhaust pipe. With a roar, the bus disappears around the corner. There's probably another bus stop at the end of the next street. I run all out to the corner in time to see the bus leave the stop at the end of the street too.

I slow down to catch my breath. I'm in an area now that has really high class homes. I don't know what to do. I could get out of this residential area and try catching another taxi ride, but he might drive me straight to the police station without stopping for red lights. A hundred thousand dollars is a lot of money.

As I go by a big house with a brick archway next to the sidewalk, a boy on a bike shoots out of the driveway. He can't see me until it's too late. He runs right into me and knocks me down. He goes down too and his bike slides across the sidewalk into the street.

"Are you hurt?"

He jumps up and examines his knee where the denim of his jeans is scuffed.

I'm banged up a little and I'm discouraged because I missed the bus. I just lay on the sidewalk for a few seconds.

"Please tell me that you aren't hurt too bad. My dad will kill me if I've really hurt you." He's starting to cry big tears. He wipes them away with a pudgy fist that doesn't look extremely clean.

"I think I'll survive, but if you don't get your bike out of the street, a car is going to run over it."

"I don't care. I don't want to ride that old thing anymore. It's a girl's bike. It belonged to my sister April before she went away to college. Clunky old thing. It's even got a basket. Dad's going to get me a new one."

"I'll tell you what. If you don't want it, I'll give you twenty dollars for it."

"If you say you aren't hurt, you can have it. I don't want it anymore. I couldn't stop; the brakes must be bad and it's all scratched up anyway."

"No, I'm not hurt. Thank you for the bike. Are you sure your dad won't mind if you give it to me?"

"No he doesn't care. He was going to take it to the Salvation Army."

If I get on the bike here, this is where the dogs will think the trail ends and they'll question the people in this house. I'm in a hurry when I wheel the bike all the way down the street, around the corner, then onto someone's lawn. It's a hassle, but it might throw them off the track. This is a nice house too. I walk around their garage, scuffing my feet to leave lots of scent. When I'm satisfied that I've done enough to confuse the dogs, I fill my water bottle at their outside spigot. I hear sirens, but it will take the dogs a few minutes to track me this far. They wouldn't be on my trail already if that darned taxi driver hadn't ratted on me. I hop on the bike and get to heck out of there fast. Unless they can follow bike tire tracks, I'm not leaving a trail that even the dogs can read.

That garage is now the end of the trail. I can picture it surrounded by an FBI SWAT team while the dogs bark.

I circle around and head back the other way. I cross the street two blocks from where I jumped out of the cab. I hope they think I continued in the other direction. I feel as if people are staring at me, but probably it's only my imagination. I stick to back streets and I don't see any police cruisers.

CHAPTER 24

When I get out of the city a little way, I pedal faster. I've got to find a place to spend the night and I'm in a hurry. If I can find a barn, or even a shed that looks as if it isn't being used, it would work for one night. I don't see anything, and I'm starting to get worried. I'm pedaling really fast now and I know I won't be able to keep this pace going forever. This bike doesn't feel very stable. Maybe the kid was right. Maybe there *is* something wrong with it. Slow down. It's still early. You'll find something. Talking to myself doesn't help much. I'm still worried and as I fly down a little hill, the back of my bike wants to move sideways. Before I can get stopped, I pretty much lose control. I end up in the ditch. My bike is lying flat and I'm sprawled on top of it. It doesn't take an expert to determine that it now has a flat tire. After careful examination, I think I know what happened. The tire is fine, but the valve stem is cracked and broken. Maybe it happened when the boy ran into me.

I've only had this bike for a little while but I already can see what an asset it is. Not only can I travel fast on it; the dogs can't follow me. I'm not ready to give up on it yet. All it needs is a new inner tube and some air. I know where there's a Walmart. They must have inner tubes. I can stuff it into the tire myself, and their service department would put some air in it for me. I've only got two new problems. Getting my bike to Walmart, which is all the way back in town, and not being recognized. I try not to get discouraged as I start wheeling my crippled bike back along the road I just traveled over.

After pushing my bike for about a mile, I'm getting tired. I'm tempted to push it out of sight into the bushes and walk to Walmart. If I do that, I'll have to buy a tire pump to put air in it and I don't want to spend any more money than I have to. The ditch is muddy here and I have to push my bike on the edge of the road. I'm hit by a rare good idea. That mud would make a good disguise. I rub some of it on my clothes and then smear it on my face. Maybe people will think I got it on me when my bike flipped. The dirt on my face should keep people from recognizing me no matter what they think.

A pickup truck pulls over in front of me and stops. Actually, it's a white Honda Ridgeline. I ignore it and push my bike on past it. It pulls ahead of me and stops again. Now what's this jerk up to? He can't recognize me with all this mud on my face. Before I can decide what to do, a little old lady with white hair climbs out of the truck.

"Got trouble, huh?"

"Just a flat tire. I'm okay."

"There aren't many houses along here. Do you live close?"

"I'll be okay. I'll get it fixed."

"How are you going to get it fixed?"

"A new inner tube."

"There aren't going to be any new inner tubes around here. Let's put it in my truck and I'll give you a ride."

"No. I'll be okay."

"Look kid! You're supposed to respect your elders. Now grab the other end of that thing and help me load it," she says as she lowers the tailgate.

Her truck has a short little bed, but it's big enough for my bike, after she moves her fishing rod and tackle box aside.

"Been up to the reservoir fishing. Caught six nice ones too, but I threw them all back. Get in the truck."

She climbs in the driver's side. She looks harmless enough, and she isn't any bigger than me, so I get in. I hope we aren't headed for the police station.

"I don't even know you."

"No, you don't, but I've got a pretty good idea who you are. I saw you smearing mud on your face."

"Where are you taking me?"

"Well first, I'm going to take you to my house and get you cleaned up and fed, then you're going to tell me what happened. After that, we'll decide what to do."

"I guess you're pretty sure you know who I am, huh?"

"Haven't got a doubt in the world. I do read the paper, you know."

"You going for the reward?"

"No."

"You don't have your seatbelt on."

"I've been driving for 60 years without a seatbelt and I'm not going to start now. Besides, they can't take my driver's license anyway."

"Why not?"

"Because they wouldn't give me one. I couldn't pass the physical."

"That's comforting." I say under my breath.

"It wasn't the hearing test that I flunked."

CHAPTER 25

I'm praying that we don't go to the police station, and it works; we don't. Her beautiful big old house is at the end of a long driveway. It's on the edge of town, but there aren't any other houses close by. There's a small vegetable garden to the left of the house. Beyond the field in back of the house is forest. It wasn't a very long ride to her house, and by the time we get there, all I've learned is that her name is Mrs. Albert, and where in the reservoir you can find the biggest fish. She drives into the garage and the big door closes behind us.

"Who else is here?"

"No one. I live alone. You aren't really a murderer are you?"

"No. I…"

"Don't tell me now. We'll talk later. I've always made snap judgments about people and I'm very seldom wrong. It's time for dinner. Let's get something to eat."

The interior of the house is beautiful too. Before I follow her into her kitchen, I take my running shoes off. She gets two big potatoes from a vegetable bin in the refrigerator and puts them in the sink.

"Peel those," she says as she hands me a peeler. "Put the peelings in this compost bucket."

While I'm busy with the potatoes, she gets carrots that I assume came from the garden and puts them in a pan. After I've finished peeling and washing the potatoes, she chops them up and puts them in another pan.

"I'm hungry and they cook a lot faster if you cut them up smaller."

She walks down the hall and comes back with some sweatpants and a shirt. She hands them to me.

"My bedroom is downstairs. You go upstairs and choose one of the bedrooms up there. Pick one that has a bathroom and take a shower. There are towels in the closets beside the lavatories and new hairbrushes and toothbrushes in the drawers. I'm equipped for guests, even though I very seldom have any. Lock the bedroom door since you don't know me yet."

There are four bedrooms upstairs. The doors are all closed and they're all clean and beautiful. There's a bathroom in the hall, but two of the bedrooms have bathrooms attached. I choose the one at the back of the house. I go in, lock the door behind me, and look around. It's definitely a girl's room. It has light blue wallpaper with pink and yellow flowers on it. The bedspread matches the wallpaper. The carpet is white and I have to be extra careful not to get mud on it. The window overlooks the woods. This bedroom is on the second floor, but it's not too high. I could climb out the window and escape if I had to.

I go into the bathroom and lock that door too. There's a hamper, but I don't want to get it dirty. I take my muddy clothes off and wrap them in my not too dirty shirt. I listen to make sure that the door isn't being unlocked while I take a good long shower. When I put on her sweats, I notice that they smell like my clothes at home. Fabric softener. I brush my hair, and even my teeth. This is the cleanest I've felt in a long time.

When I open the bedroom door, there's a fan running downstairs and dinner smells wonderful. My nose leads me down the stairs. A grill is built into Mrs. Albert's kitchen stove, and two steaks are sizzling on it.

"My late husband had some cows and I like to support the industry, and besides, I like steak. What do you want to drink? We've got milk, juice, and water."

"Water please."

"You'll have to get it yourself. There's water in the sink and the refrigerator door has water and ice. There are glasses in the cupboard to the left of the sink. While you're up, please get me a beer from the fridge. I'll drink it right from the can."

I hadn't realized how hungry I was but I ate the whole steak along with a potato and lots of carrots. While we're eating Mrs. Albert talks about fishing and how she should have brought a couple of fish home, but she was too lazy to clean them. Then she told me how she was trying to limit her beer drinking to one can a day.

"My late husband got me started drinking beer and now I like the stuff. Don't you ever start drinking beer."

After we finish eating and cleaning up, we sit back down at the table, and she becomes serious.

"Tell me about your life. Everything up to this incident."

While I tell her my whole life, she keeps asking me questions. She seems particularly interested in my involvement in the church.

"Are you sure that you want me to tell you all this stuff? It must be pretty boring for someone who has lived so much more than I have."

"Just because someone has lived longer doesn't necessarily mean that they've lived more. Keep talking."

Finally I get to the part where mom was depressed. I'm crying when I stop. At this point, she doesn't sympathize or comment.

"Now, tell me what happened."

I wipe my eyes with a paper napkin, and tell her everything that happened starting with the confrontation in the lunch room. She didn't interrupt me or say anything while I was telling this part of my story.

She looked serious when she said, "That story is a lot different from what I read in the paper."

"I know. I'm in real trouble."

"You sure are. They've got lots of witnesses and juries rely heavily on witnesses."

"But they're lying."

"All of them?"

"No. Just the two boys. The girls couldn't hear what the boys were saying, so they don't know what was going on."

"Why would the boys lie?"

"To protect themselves and Todd. They probably thought I'd accuse them of rape."

"Wouldn't you have?"

"Probably not."

"Why not?"

"I didn't actually get raped, and besides, they're football heroes and everyone loves them. I'm new here and I don't have any friends. No one would have believed me."

"You're right, and the jury won't believe you either."

"That's why I escaped."

"How *did* you escape? You're such a little thing, how did you do it?"

Then I told her the whole story of how I escaped. I told her that I never would have been able to do it if I hadn't been good at gymnastics and that I was in really good physical condition.

"Where were you going on your bicycle?"

"I was looking for a shed or a barn. Some place where I could spend the night."

"Would you like to spend the night here?"

"Yes, but I couldn't."

"Why not."

"You'd be aiding a fugitive. That's a serious crime, especially if the fugitive is a murderer."

"They'd have to prove that I knew you were a fugitive. Anyway, you're not going anywhere tonight. Consider yourself kidnapped. Have you watched all of the Star Wars episodes?"

"No."

"Well that's what we're going to do tonight. We're going to start watching Star Wars. I'm going to town and get the CD's right now."

"What am I going to do?"

"Stay here and check the place out."

"You don't even know me; I could rob you blind."

"As near as I can tell, you haven't told me a single lie. I told you that I'm a good judge of character. Besides, you haven't got any wheels and you couldn't sell anything anyway."

CHAPTER 26

When the big garage door creaks open, I'm asleep on the couch. As I run to the window in the kitchen door that goes to the garage, Mrs. Albert drives in. No police or FBI. She's alone. While the garage door closes, I walk back to the couch and sit down before she sees me spying on her. I'm rubbing the sleep out of my eyes when she comes in.

"You don't look as if you're up for watching much TV tonight. That's okay. Go to bed. We'll start watching it tomorrow. I got you a few clothes." She gives me a bag.

"There's a nightgown and some pajamas in there. Take your pick. There are also a few other things. Lock your bedroom door. You'll sleep better."

The few other things turned out to be jeans, a shirt, and some underclothes and socks. This is too good to be true. I hope she doesn't get into trouble.

It's wonderful to crawl into this clean, comfortable, queen-sized bed. I lie on my back and stretch out my arms and legs. This bed is way bigger than I need. It makes me feel extravagant, almost wasteful. It's great.

I'm afraid I'm letting my guard down. Mrs. Albert is so down-to-earth, so open, so...nice. I don't even know her, but it's hard not to trust her. I drift off, then wake with a start. Everything is quiet. Nothing is wrong.

When I wake, it's morning. Sunlight is flooding my room. My room? I must be dreaming. It's quiet. Too quiet. Something must be wrong. I quietly slide out of bed and look out the window. No FBI. I tiptoe to the door, unlock it and crack it open. Not a sound. After listening for a few minutes, I close and lock it again. Finally, I go into my bathroom. My bathroom.

When I finally work up enough courage, I quietly descend the stairs while savoring the aroma of hazelnut coffee. Mrs. Albert is sitting at the table reading the paper.

"Well, you still haven't been caught," she says without looking up. "The mayor is really putting the pressure on though. I'm going to have ham and eggs and grits for breakfast. What about you?"

"Mrs. Albert you've been wonderful to me, but this is wrong. I'm taking advantage of you and you could get in serious trouble for helping me. If I could take advantage of you one more time and ask you to help me get an inner tube for my bike tire, I'd go and stop imposing on your kindness."

"Well, that was quite a speech. I told you. You've been kidnapped. What do you want for breakfast? Could you eat what I'm having?"

"But..."

"No buts. You have to cook the eggs. You *can* fry eggs can't you?"

"Yes."

CHAPTER 27

It takes us several days to watch the whole Star Wars series. I make a lot of popcorn and Mrs. Albert drinks a lot of beer. Considerably more than one can per day. It never seems to affect her much, though. I've come to like her very much, although I'm trying not to let myself get too close to her. I know this is too good to last, and besides, I feel guilty for taking advantage of her.

"Mrs. Albert, I don't like imposing on you like this. There isn't even anything I can do to contribute and I'm putting you in danger by staying here. I should be thinking about leaving before someone finds out that I'm here."

"How are they going to find out about you? And besides, you do lots of things to help me. You cook and clean, you work in the garden, and you help me in lots of other ways."

"I don't help much at all. I wish there were something that I could do that would really be a help. I can't do anything, though."

"Of course you can do things. You must have talents or things that you like to do because you're good at them. What *can* you do besides just being very beautiful?"

I can feel myself blushing. I can't help it.

"Nothing that's worth anything."

"Like what?"

"Well, I can sing, and I can draw and paint, but what good is that?"

"Yes, I remember you told me that you like to do drawings and paintings, and I think I've got the perfect project for an artist to help me with."

"What is it?"

"Well, I don't really have any family left, but I do have a granddaughter that I'm very fond of. I've been thinking of having a piece of jewelry made for her. Something unique. Something simple, elegant, and in keeping with her Christian faith. I just can't think of what it should be. You're an artist, so maybe you can come up with an idea. Think about it."

I do think about it, and by the next morning, I have an idea. I draw it on a notepad, but although I really like it, I know it would have to be custom made. It would be too expensive.

Mrs. Albert confronts me at breakfast.

"Have you had any ideas about a piece of jewelry?"

"Well, I've made my first attempt, but it's not going to work."

"Why not? Did you draw it?"

"Yes, here it is."

I show her the notepad. It's a necklace. A gold cross with a ruby at each spot where the nails were driven through Christ's hands and feet, and a diamond in the center.

"The rubies symbolize blood where the nails were driven, and the diamond in the center symbolizes purity. The stones would all be expensive though, and the gold cross would have to be quite thick to set them deeply enough. Otherwise they'd get caught on sweaters. And the chain would have to go crosswise, so the cross would always face outward. All that stuff would make it really expensive. You probably wouldn't be able to get anyone to make it anyway. I'll keep thinking, and I'll come up with something more practical in a day or two."

"Don't bother. I love it, and I think I know someone who would make it. His name is Stanley and he has a shop in a flea market over in Wilmington."

"In a flea market?"

"Yes, a flea market. You'll see."

CHAPTER 28

Mrs. Albert has scanned my drawing and e-mailed it to the guy in Wilmington. He told her he'd have it finished in about ten days. She's really excited. In some ways, she's like a little kid. She's pretty old though, and I'm worried about her health. She takes a lot of pills. I try to help her all I can. She goes out to play cards with some of her friends and when I'm alone, I clean. I've cleaned this whole house, one room at a time, although I didn't find anything that was very dirty. She told me not to bother because she has someone do it twice a year. I do it anyway. I have to do something to help pay my way. I even worked on the attic some and I've weeded the whole garden.

She acts as if I'm going to stay here forever, but I know that's not going to work. Eventually, someone would find out that I'm here and then she'd be in trouble. I told her again that we were going to have to think about my leaving. She said that she has an appointment with her lawyer in a few weeks and she'd ask him about me. She said that he would know what my best defense would be if I go to court and that it would be illegal for him to report me. She says that after she talks to him, we'll come up with a plan.

I try to do everything I can think of to help her, but I still feel as though I'm taking advantage of her. Although I've fought it, I feel very close to her, and she trusts me completely. She went fishing again a couple of days ago, and when she came home, her truck was muddy. Yesterday, I backed it out of the garage so that I could wash it. My bike wasn't in the back. She must have taken it to get the tire fixed. Anyway, I could have stolen her truck and ran, but she wasn't concerned at all. I was never very close to my own grandmother, but I sure envy Mrs. Albert's granddaughter.

I walk into the living room with a cup of tea for her and she's on the phone. She motions for me to put the tea on the coffee table and to sit on the couch.

"I know we have an appointment in a couple of weeks, but I need to see you now."

"Stewart Ames. You've been my lawyer for forty years and you know that I wouldn't request a meeting on such short notice if it weren't important."

"Okay. Two this afternoon."

She hangs up.

"Well thank you for the tea. You're always so considerate. I've got to go to town to see my lawyer this afternoon and I'll stop at the grocery store on the way home, so I may be late."

"Okay. Please try to make it home before dark, though, or I'll worry about you."

I've been doing the cooking, and we eat really well. Mrs. Albert goes grocery shopping every few days and the refrigerator and cupboards are always full. We have steak pretty often, along with all the fixings. There's exercise equipment in the attic and I work out every day. If I didn't, I'd look like a blimp. Mrs. Albert doesn't exercise at all. I don't know how she stays so slim.

CHAPTER 29

It's Saturday afternoon when the phone rings. I'm in the kitchen, but I can hear Mrs. Albert's side of the conversation. I listen because I'm always worried when the phone rings. It's okay, though, because I can tell that it's the guy from Wilmington. After she hangs up, she hurries into the kitchen. She's talking fast. I know she's excited.

"He said that he really liked the necklace and that he got so caught up in the project that he couldn't stop. They...It's all done. I want to go over right now and get it."

"It's late. It would be dark before you got home. Driving after dark can be dangerous if you don't do it very much."

"You're right. The flea market is open both Saturday and Sunday. We'll leave first thing in the morning."

"I can't go with you. Someone might recognize me."

"I really want you to go. We'll think of something."

The next morning, we don't take time to cook anything. We just eat cold cereal for breakfast because Mrs. Albert is so anxious to get going.

"My truck has tinted windows. No one could see you very well, but I think we should dress you up as if you were my sister just in case."

"That's a great idea. Have you got any big hats?"

"I've got lots of hats. You can take your pick. I don't wear them much anymore, but I've got some pretty ones."

The trip to Wilmington is uneventful, but I'm nervous because she always drives too fast. When we pull through the gate at the flea market we find ourselves at the end of a line of cars that are shuffling into parking places. The place is packed. Most of the tables are outside, but there's also a big building. We find a place to park and I stay in the truck while she goes into the building. It's a good thing that I brought a book, because it's a long time before I see her coming out of the building. She has a big smile on her face.

"That Stanley sure likes to talk, but he's really talented. Look at this."

She hands me an envelope with the necklace inside. I open it and the gold necklace slides into my hand. It's beautiful. I had my doubts about fine jewelry being made by some guy in a flea market, but Mrs. Albert sure knew what she was talking about. The necklace is perfect.

"Look at the back."

I read the inscription.

"Vicky love Gram A."

"Wow! Your granddaughter's name is Vicky?"

"Sure is. Here, let me put it on."

When she reaches over to put it around my neck, it hits me that she has had the necklace made for me. I start crying as I pull her frail body to me.

"Now how can I fasten this thing with you hugging me and blubbering all over the place?"

I hug her even tighter.

"And furthermore, you have a choice. You can call me either Ivy, or Grammy. Forget the Mrs. Albert business."

"Grammy. I'll never take it off."

I hardly know my grandmother in Maine, and I don't feel at all disloyal. This Grammy never wears any jewelry, but she gives me another envelope, and inside is an identical necklace.

"Now put this one on me. Wearing the same necklace will make us even closer. Stanley wanted my permission to make some more of these to sell, but I said no. I want them to be unique."

We have to wait in a long line to get out of the flea market. Even after we get on the road, I'm still emotional. For some reason, memories of mom come back as strong as ever. Then I think about my wonderful new Grammy and how impossible our situation is. If only I weren't a fugitive.

On the way back, although I wouldn't have thought it possible with her driving, I fall asleep. I don't wake up until she stops to get us some Subway sandwiches and a couple of Dr. Peppers. I know she really wanted a beer, but she didn't get one.

CHAPTER 30

This morning when I wake up, it's cloudy and the breeze coming through my open window is actually cool. I check the laptop that Grammy gave me. A dreary day is predicted, but no rain. There won't be many people on the trail today. This would be a good day to go for a run. I usually cook breakfast, but this morning, Grammy has it all cooked when I go downstairs. Everything is already on the table, so I sit down.

"Grammy, there won't be many people on the jogging trail today and it's been a long time since I've had a real run. Is there any chance that you'd take me up to the trail and wait for me to run? It would be about an hour."

"Your bike was in the shop, but I picked it up the other day. It's on the back of the truck. You could just go for a bike ride."

"That was really nice of you. The tire was still okay wasn't it?"

"I don't know about the tire, but I know that your bike is okay now."

"I could go for a bike ride, and I need to check it out anyway, but today, I feel as if I need to run."

"I don't know where the trail is, but if you can show me, I'll take you. I've got a hard Sudoku that I can work on. How are you going to keep from being recognized?"

"Before, I put my hair up and wore a cap and sunglasses. If I start and stop running somewhere along the trail and not at the beginning, no one will notice me."

I go back upstairs and when I come back down, I'm wearing my running shorts and shoes, the prison gym top with my gold cross under it, my Gold Trucking cap, and sunglasses. I'm carrying the prison pajama top to put on after my run when I'm all sweaty. The same clothes I had on the last time I ran. I even have my twenty-dollar bill in my sneaker, for luck.

"We've got to get you some new clothes to run in."

"These are fine Grammy. I'm not trying for a fashion statement."

When we get to the starting spot for the trail, we keep going up the road until we find a spot for Grammy to pull off the road, then I cut through the woods to the trail, and stretch a little. I mark the spot on the trail with a branch and start running. I was right, there aren't very many people on the trail.

I can tell right off that it's been too long since I've run. I'm slow. After a while, I limber up and do better, but I'm mad at myself. I'm out of shape. I run for an hour, and when I get back to the truck, I'm as out of breath as I should have been if I'd run a lot faster. I've got to do something about this. I thought exercising in the attic would help, but it doesn't seem to have helped much. I'm sweaty, and I put my prison pajama top back on.

"Grammy, I'm in terrible shape."

"I guess you don't want to stop at the DQ on the way home and get a Blizzard, huh?"

"I need to forget about Blizzards. I'm going to have to either start running, or stop eating. I'm so out of shape, I should do both."

Grammy has a hard time getting her truck turned around, but after we get going, she seems okay. Before we get to the place where there's a sharp turn by the boulders on the riverbank, though, I know we're going too fast.

"Grammy. Slow down."

I look at her and her eyes are closed and her head droops. We're going faster.

"Grammy!!"

I try to grab the steering wheel, but my seatbelt won't let me. I cover my face as we leave the road. There's a loud crash and we're flying through the air. Then there's another crash. The airbag hits me and the smell of gunpowder, or whatever they use to inflate the airbags, makes it hard for me to breathe. We stop on top of the big rocks. Grammy has a lot of blood coming from her mouth and she doesn't move at all.

"Grammy!!"

I unhook my seatbelt and try to compress her chest. It feels hard and her mouth is full of blood. Her left arm is almost completely severed and blood is running from the stub, but it's not spurting. Her heart isn't beating. I try to compress her chest again, then tip her head to get the blood to drain from her mouth, but it's no use.

"Grammy! Why wouldn't you wear a seatbelt?"

I keep trying to get some air into her lungs and I even pound on her chest to try to get her heart going again, but it doesn't work. Finally, I give up. It's obvious that she's dead. I'm sick. I don't know what to do. I'm crying really hard. I loved Grammy and she was the only one who loved me.

A lady has stopped in the road behind us. She's talking on her cellphone. I've got to get out of here. I haven't got time for this crying. I'll do that later. My sunglasses have come off, but they're lying on the dashboard. I wipe my eyes with my sleeve, and put them back on, Then, I pick up my hat and put it on, making sure that it's straight. My prison pajama top has Grammy's blood all over it, but it's dark color keeps the spattered blood from showing up very much. I crawl out through the hole where the window on my side broke out. The little rock salt-like pieces prick my hands, but barely break the skin.

My bike is in the back of the truck again, only it's not my bike. The bike I pull out of the truck is a top-of-the-line mountain bike. The only thing that's familiar is the basket from my old bike. I head toward town. I've got to stop crying. My sunglasses are fogging up. This thing really flies.

"Thank you Grammy for the new bike."

When I hear a siren, I pull off the road and push my new bike into the woods. I can't really get out of sight because the briers are so thick. The state police cruiser passes me going at least a hundred. He probably wouldn't have seen me if I had been standing in the middle of the road. I push my bike back out of the woods and continue on to town.

CHAPTER 31

I've got to find a place to spend the night, but I haven't got any good ideas. I don't think my disguise is very good. I can't let people see me up close. It's easy to pedal my new bike fast, and at this speed, people aren't going to get a very good look at me.

As I go by a side street, a lady with shiny black hair is walking away from me. My mom, is the first thought that comes into my head. Even her blue dress looks like one of mom's. My brakes are involuntarily applied so quickly that the bike's rear wheel drags. Even so, I'm going so fast that I go right by the side street. I know it's not her, but I can't help it. I have to see her face. By the time I get turned around and headed down the side street, she's out of sight. I pedal like mad down to the intersection and spot her going into a mall.

A lot of people are walking on the sidewalk so I fly down the street. As irrational as it is, I can't let her get away. When I catch up with her, of course she looks nothing like mom. I'd like to find a corner and cry, but the fear of being caught spurs me on. I ride to the outside edge of the parking lot where there aren't any people.

Beside the fence is a recycle bin. Apparently, it's full because there are bags and boxes stacked all along the front. I park the bike out of sight behind it. It smells like urine back here, but it's dry. I hold my necklace and say a prayer for Mom. Then I say one for Grammy, both Grammys.

After I've got my emotions under control a little better, I reach around the corner, and pull the closest bag behind the bin. I'm out of sight of the mall when I check its contents. It's stuffed full of clothes that obviously belonged to a very large woman. Disappointed, I put it back and pull out another one. It has mostly boy's clothes in it; they look clean, though. A pair of worn jeans looks about my size. I pull them on over my shorts. They fit okay, a little tight. I wouldn't need a belt. I take my twenty-dollar bill out of my sneaker and stuff it into my pocket. I like having pockets. I like wearing jeans. Maybe I should be a boy. Not a chance, but maybe I should look like a boy. I look for a shirt that a girl wouldn't wear. I settle on an equally worn-looking jean shirt with a big stain on one sleeve.

I check out the rest of the bag's contents, but nothing else looks interesting except a couple of pairs of thin nylon shorts that I could use for underwear and a nice pair of socks. I put those in the basket of my bike. The shirt fits okay when I try it on, so I stuff the prison pajama top into the bag. That should be a fair trade.

Next, I reach around and pull a box out. It has lots of interesting things in it. Books, shoes, cheap jewelry, a nice pen and pencil set; I'm only interested in two things. A tiny makeup kit and the paints and brushes of an acrylic paint set. The brushes are in good shape, and hardly any of the paint has been used. I usually paint with oils, but acrylics dry faster and you can paint on anything. It's probably stupid to keep them, but I really like to paint, and I can't pass them up. I stuff them all into the socks that I saved.

I check out the makeup kit. I don't think it's ever been used. It has a little mirror. I darken my complexion a little and add some shadows by my nose and eyes. A tiny line on each side and just the hint of a mustache makes my mouth a little wider. Being an artist really helps. I turn my cap around so my hair won't fall out the hole in the back. After I make sure it's piled on top of my head and not sticking out around the edges, I take another look in the mirror and a boy stares back at me.

CHAPTER 32

Feeling like the invisible man, I skirt the mall and continue pedaling. A sign on the window of a little diner reminds me how hungry I am. "Red Hot Hot Dogs. 2 for $1.50."

There are no other customers, and the lady behind the counter doesn't even look up.

"Two hot dogs please." I try to keep my voice low and slow.

"They're in the steamer." She points.

"Could I have some water?"

Since the diner is empty, I have my choice of where to sit. I choose a booth where I can watch my bike. My new bike is really something. Graphite frame, the whole works. If anyone stole it, I'd be some upset.

I look at the paper plate under my hot dogs and have an idea.

"Can I have another paper plate?"

"Knock yourself out." She's trying to hide the fact that she's smoking in spite of the sign.

I get another plate and then go out and get my paints and brushes.

"Can I have a paper cup?"

She doesn't say anything. Just slides one across the counter. I pour in half my water. Another good thing about acrylic paints. Water cleanup.

By the time I've finished my hot dogs, I'm too far along with my painting to stop. There still aren't any customers, and she isn't hurrying me out the door, so I keep going.

When I'm finally done, I hide my signature V in the

painting. Then I wash my brushes, put the caps back on the paint tubes, study the painting one last time, and cry. After hurrying into the restroom, I blot the tears away before they ruin the paint job on my face.

When I come out of the restroom, the waitress is studying the painting of my Mom. I've captured her sad smile. I can't look at it again.

"What are you going to do with this painting?" The waitress is a pretty Latino lady.

"I don't know. I can't look at it without crying. It's my Mom."

"Where is she?"

"She died."

"I'm so sorry. She's beautiful. She's obviously Mexican."

"Yes, we're from Juarez."

"So am I. Could you sell it?"

"I don't know."

"I know it should be worth a lot more, but I could give you whatever you want that's on the menu and twenty dollars for it."

CHAPTER 33

I've got to stop thinking about my Mom and Grammy. Crying's going to mess up my disguise. I've been trying to shake this mood, but I still feel really sad. I did manage to eat a pepper steak sandwich and a milkshake, though, on top of the two hot dogs.

I'm in a rundown section of town when I see a "ROOMS FOR RENT" sign. If I could sell a few paintings, maybe I could rent a room if it were cheap enough. I may as well check on prices. I won't be able to see my bike if I leave it in the street, so I wheel it into the lobby. I lean it against the wall and look for an office or manager. All I see is a mail slot with a sign. "RENT."

I'm getting my bike turned around ready to leave, when a girl with a blue and orange backpack on her back and an envelope in her hand comes out of the door marked 103. Her eyes are red, and I can tell that she's been crying.

"Are you okay?"

"Yes, I'm okay now. I'm going home."

"How do you rent a room here?"

"You bang on the door over the sign, and sometimes the building manager is in there."

"Could you tell me how much the rooms are here?"

"They're twenty dollars a week or fifty dollars a month. There's also a twenty dollar deposit."

"I've got forty dollars, but I hate to spend it all. Maybe I can find something cheaper."

"You might, but I doubt it. These rooms aren't much. I'll tell you what, though. There are over three weeks left on my room and I'm leaving. If you want it, you can have it for twenty. That way, I won't have to fight with him for my deposit."

"Do you mind if I look?"

"Heck no."

The room is small. Everything is a drab pale yellowish green except the gray floor. There's a bed, a chair, and a nightstand with a lamp. One small window faces the bare brick wall of the building next door. Instead of a closet there's a short piece of iron pipe stretched across one back corner with a couple of clothes hangers on it. A cheap full-length mirror hangs on the inside of the door. I move the chair exposing a wastebasket.

"There's a dumpster out back."

She's right, it's not much, but there's enough space for my bike and it's on the first floor. It's also clean.

"Where's the bathroom?"

"Second door on the right. I'm sorry that there aren't any bedclothes. I gave all my bedding to the girl in 102. There's still a pillow, though."

I give her twenty dollars and she hands me the envelope with the key inside.

"Good luck."

"Thanks."

After she leaves I slide the key out of the envelope and put it in my pocket. It reminds me of sliding my necklace out of an envelope. I sit on the bed holding my necklace and think of Grammy lying dead in her truck. I cry for a long time.

I check out the pipe across the back corner. I don't have any clothes to hang on it, but it looks strong enough to hold me while I'm doing chin-ups and pull-ups. That's good, because I expect that it's going to be hard to get enough exercise. I do a few chin-ups just to make sure the pipe is solid enough.

I empty the basket of my bike and put the stuff on the nightstand, then I head back to the recycle bin. I need some bedclothes and I remember seeing some blankets in one of the boxes there.

CHAPTER 34

It's starting to get dark when I get back to the recycle bin and although it's lit by a streetlight, for some reason, I don't feel as exposed as I paw through the stuff. In the bottom of the box with the blankets, along with some towels, is a backpack. My next big find is a bag of old lady's clothes that are small enough to fit me. There's also a big floppy hat. When I dressed like an old lady with Grammy I thought it was a great disguise. I stuff the whole thing into the backpack and put the blankets and towels in the basket of my bike.

That night I wrap a towel around my head in case I meet someone in the hall. I head to the bathroom to try to turn my face into an old lady. The lamp in my room is too dim for a serious makeup job. Even though I think I can pull off the granny deception, when I leave in the morning, I'm a boy again. I'm looking for a good place to market my paintings and I need to ride my bike. Not a good idea if I'm an old lady.

By the time I've checked all the streets that are close enough to walk to in my old lady clothes, I'm discouraged. There were a couple of good spots, but they were occupied. One had a lady selling flowers, and the other one had an old man with a cup who was just begging. I don't want to compete with anyone.

I'm hungry, but I've decided not to cash my last twenty unless it's a real emergency. I've checked this street before, but this time I strike pay dirt. I found the spot before, but I didn't think I'd feel okay here. Too high-class. The stores and shops are expensive and there are Cadillacs and Mercedes parked at the curb. This time, there's a guy in the spot. I don't know why he is allowed to be here; he's sitting on a stool in the mouth of a wide alley, playing a violin. He looks clean and well dressed. A hand-painted sign says 'Steve Ward veteran.' An upturned hat on the sidewalk contains a few dollars. His playing sounds good. Maybe he'll let me share his spot. I wouldn't really be competing.

Now I need a painting to sell. I head back to my supply depot, better known as a recycle bin. When I get there, I'm disappointed. They've made a pickup. Everything's gone except one box. I soon discover why it's sitting in front of the bin. The thing's too darned heavy. Most people couldn't lift it high enough to put it through the door. It contains cooking dishes, including several heavy cast-iron frying pans. There are also three Teflon-coated aluminum ones with most of the coating worn off and some stainless steel pots.

At first, I'm disappointed, but the backs of the aluminum frying pans are shiny. I could paint on those. If I could sell a paper plate, maybe I can sell a frying pan. I put them in the basket of my bike, along with a stainless steel pan cover that I might be able to paint on.

When I get back to my room, I get my paints organized and start painting. Although that little squirrel really had me scared, he was pretty. It's fun painting him, and by the time I go to sleep, I have captured my squirrel on the back of a frying pan along with a little hidden signature V. I'm happy with my painting. He looks alive, although his whiskers aren't moving.

CHAPTER 35

I slept like a rock last night in spite of the racket coming from the room over mine. I'm not as afraid of getting caught every minute, now. My disguises are going to work. The mirror in the bathroom is a big help when I'm working on my face. I think I'm going to be okay.

I'm still pretty hungry, though. Selling a frying pan is my top priority. I touch up my boy's face, wheel my bike out to the sidewalk, and ride over to the next block to see if the man with the violin is there. He isn't, but I'm not too disappointed. He didn't show up yesterday until sometime in the afternoon.

I decide to go back and paint another frying pan while I'm waiting. I go around the block the other direction on the way back. I pass a diner and almost weaken and spend some of my emergency money. Whenever I'm tempted to feel sorry for myself because running is so hard I remind myself that if I'm caught, the two options are life in prison, or the death penalty. That kind of brings things back into perspective.

The second squirrel is taking just as long to paint. I think it's going to be as pretty as the first one, but it isn't as fun. I've painted the frying pans so the squirrels will be right side up when the frying pans are hung by the hole in the handle. I hang one of them on a nail where one of the previous tenants hung something on the wall. It looks really good to me. I hope someone agrees enough to buy it.

I decide to go for a bike ride while I'm waiting for the violin man. I need to check out the area and I need to get some exercise too. I'm not going to get too carried away with the exercise part while I'm hungry, though.

Five blocks over, I come to a street that has trash piled up by the sidewalk, waiting for pickup. On top of a stack of boxes and old magazines, is a hotplate. Ellen was a friend of mine in Albuquerque and her folks had one just like it. It's an induction cooker, really cool. The pot gets hot, but not the hotplate. The only problem with it is that it won't work with aluminum pots. For it to work, the cookware has to be magnetic. This one probably doesn't work at all, but who knows, it might. I look around to see if anyone will see me picking the dump. When I don't see anyone; I can't resist putting the hotplate in my basket. I hurry home with my potential treasure.

Back at the room, I discover that there is only one outlet in the whole room. It's the one the lamp plugs into, and it's under the bed. I move the bed out and plug my new hotplate in. The light flickers and goes out. I jiggle the plug and the light flickers. If I hold the plug just right, the light stays on. Shouldn't be too serious. I've seen dad work on a problem like this; I should be able to get it working. Just because the light comes on, doesn't mean that it will work, but I'm betting that it will. I hop on my bike and pedal back to the recycle bin supply store to get a pot to try my hotplate with.

I pick up the pot that fits the cover that I got yesterday. It's stainless steel and I'm not sure that it's magnetic enough, so I grab a cast iron frying pan while I'm there. I know that *it's* magnetic. People have brought in more stuff, but it's all inside the bin where I can't reach it.

On my way back home, I notice that the violin man

is back at his post. I hurry and apply my little old lady disguise including the big floppy hat. My long dress hides my running shoes.

Practicing talking like I think a little old lady might talk makes me feel foolish, and I feel a little silly and self-conscious as I walk over to talk to the violin man with the frying pans in my hand.

CHAPTER 36

When I get to the alley where the old man is, he has a serene look on his face while he plays on his violin. I recognize that it's an old hymn, but I can't remember the name. There are a lot of people walking by and a few of them slow down or even stop for a minute. A lady in a pink sweater stops and puts some money in his hat. I wait until he finishes playing.

"That sounded really good. I guess you've been playing for a long time."

"Yes."

He's looking at my frying pans.

"I was wondering if you'd mind if I keep you company while I try to sell these paintings."

I hold one up so he can see it.

"I'm a little nervous about standing on the street alone."

"It's a free country."

"I won't do it if you don't want me to. I've only got two of them. It might bring you more customers."

He doesn't respond.

"Could we just try it, please? If it doesn't work, I'll stop."

"Like I said, it's a free country. Knock yourself out."

"Thank you."

CHAPTER 37

I put one of the frying pans out of sight in the mouth of the alleyway and set the other one on the sidewalk in front of me. After watching people walk by for at least fifteen minutes, I'm starting to wonder if this is going to work.

Finally, a guy stops and picks up the painting.

"Did you paint this?"

"Yes."

"Very good."

He puts it back down and walks away. Well, at least, that's encouraging.

Two ladies stop to look. They discuss the painting for a few minutes.

"Did you paint it?"

"Yes I did."

"I like it very much. What was your subject?"

"Yesterday, I had a nap under a little tree. When I opened my eyes, he was sitting on a limb over my head."

"How much are you asking for it."

"I don't know. Whatever you think."

"How long did it take you?"

"About three hours, I guess."

"It must be worth more, but would you sell it for twenty five dollars?"

After the ladies leave, I pick up the other frying pan. I'm hungry and I'm going to get something to eat right away. The violin man, Mr. Ward, is watching.

"I'm going to get some lunch. Are you hungry? I've got some money."

"No. I'm not hungry."

Vicky's Escape

Once I'm home, I change back to a boy. I hurry out to find a place that has hamburgers and greasy fries. As soon as I'm not starving, I stop at a dollar store and do some grocery shopping. I get oatmeal, a tub of margarine, peanut butter, and a loaf of day-old bread. Back when I had access to a computer, I read a blurb on the internet that said that eggs don't need to be refrigerated, so I get a dozen of those too and as an afterthought, a small pack of paper plates and cups, and some soap. I hope I can get the hotplate to work.

On the way back to my room, a guy on the sidewalk has a little black and white Papillon on a leash. It runs toward me wiggling all over, just asking me to stop and say hello. I slow down and it's so friendly and happy acting that I have to stop. The guy on the other end of the leash is a big fellow. I'd guess he's only about thirty-five, but he's completely bald. He says her name is Katy and she's two years old.

After playing with her for a few minutes, I take a good look at her face. She's so beautiful that I already know that I'm going to paint her. When I leave, her tail droops a little. I'd like to take her with me. I'll never have a dog because I don't have a life. I tell myself to stop feeling sorry for myself. It doesn't do any good.

I'm rearranging my room. I slide the bed over against the back wall and put the nightstand beside it, right over the outlet. There's room for both the hotplate and lamp on the nightstand. The little light on the hotplate will stay on if I hold the cord tight against the plug. I put it in that position and push the leg of the nightstand against it. Problem solved. I'm anxious to see if the hotplate really works, but before I check it out, I do some chin-ups on the iron pipe. Doing chin-ups isn't my favorite thing, but I've got to stay in shape as best I can.

Using one of my new bars of soap, I wash my dishes. My cast iron frying pan heats up pretty fast with my hotplate on 'high.' I put a little margarine in the bottom and then a slice of bread. In no time, I have a nice slice of toast. Dad always liked toast made in a frying pan. He said a toaster dries it out too much. I think he was right. After taking the toast out, I shut the hotplate off and fry an egg before the frying pan cools off. Great. I should have bought some silverware at the dollar store though.

After I've eaten, I take a clean paper plate out of the package and start painting the little dog. Before I'm finished I'm sad. I'd love to have a little dog like that. It would be wonderful to go to bed with it and have it snuggle against me. "Stop feeling sorry for yourself and finish this painting." I have to talk to myself so I won't get depressed.

CHAPTER 38

Mr. Ward is no friendlier today, but at least he's not telling me that he doesn't want me here. I put my squirrel frying pan and my new dog on a paper plate both out on the sidewalk.

He has his violin singing a whole range of songs. I don't think I've heard him repeat any. He's really good and people are stopping to listen.

A young guy in a nice suit picks up the doggy plate. The guy looks about twenty-five.

"I'll give you ten dollars for it."

"It took me three hours to paint it."

"For that much effort, you should have used a better canvas. You did a great job though. Fifteen."

"Okay."

A while later, a pretty lady with lots of jewelry picks up the frying pan. She studies it for several minutes. While she's looking at the frying pan, I check her out. She has shiny dark hair and striking blue eyes.

"Can you do portraits?"

I think I did a good job painting my mom, so I say, "Yes, I can do portraits."

I don't want her to get a good look at my face, so I try not to look at her while she's talking to me. Instead, I study her expensive-looking shoes. It's impolite, but I don't have a choice.

"Will you take thirty dollars for this squirrel?"

"Yes."

"You did a really good job painting on this metal frying pan, can you paint on pewter?"

"I've never done it, but I don't see why not." I tell

her. I know acrylic paint will stick to almost anything.

"I've got a big pewter serving tray. Could you paint the faces of the ladies in my bridge club on it?"

"I can if I can see them or if you have a good color photograph."

"Can you meet me here in an hour?"

"Yes."

She pays me for my squirrel, then hurries back up the sidewalk.

I feel really good about all the money I've made today, although it's probably not much more than minimum wage. I can't *get* a minimum wage job, though, and besides, I don't have to pay income tax on this money.

I decide to just stay here and listen to the music while I wait for the lady to come back. The violin man finishes a song that I don't know. I think it's too hi-brow for me to be familiar with it. He pauses for a minute or two, then starts a new song. It's one of the songs that we sang in the choir at West Mesa School in Albuquerque. Without thinking, I start singing. I guess it's just a reflex.

"Oh Danny Boy, the pipes, the pipes are calling."

The violin stops and I stop too. I'm embarrassed.

"I'm sorry."

"Don't stop."

People on the sidewalk come closer and the man with the little boy repeats. "Don't stop."

I look over at Mr. Ward. He has a scowl, but he starts playing again. By the time the song is over, people are clapping and several are putting money in his hat. He quickly puts his violin in its case, picks up his stool and hat, and leaves. I'm confused and I don't know what to do. People are murmuring as they walk off.

Vicky's Escape

I don't like walking in these granny clothes, but I don't like standing on the sidewalk alone either. I slowly walk to the corner to kill time. When I get there, my watch says I still have a half hour before the lady will return. I decide to finish walking around the block.

I've completed my trip around the block and I'm halfway back to the violin-man's alley when a cop comes around the opposite corner and walks up the sidewalk toward me. I almost panic. My legs are telling me to run. He's young, but he has a potbelly and I have no doubt that even in my out-of-shape condition, I can outrun him. The trouble is, if I do, I'll blow my cover. There are usually quite a few people on this block, but at the moment, there's no crowd to blend into, just two other people on the sidewalk. If I duck into the alleyway he'll see me and be suspicious, and I can't escape into the next doorway. It's too close to him. There's no crosswalk here, so if I cross the street, he might stop me for jaywalking. I'm trapped. I just hope my disguise is good enough. I'm sweating like mad when we meet, but he doesn't even glance at me. Although it's a huge relief, it's kind of a put-down too. I'm used to guys at least noticing me.

I continue on to the corner and when I turn around he's gone and the lady who wants me to paint her serving tray is approaching from the other direction. I walk back to meet her and reach out with shaky hands to accept the tray and the envelope with pictures in it.

"Do your painting on the inside. I'm going to coat it with clear epoxy and use it when we have a bridge party. The ladies will be surprised. Can you meet me here tomorrow?"

"Better give me one more day. Portraits can take a

little longer if I'm not familiar with the subject. I'll have to study the pictures a little."

"Okay. I'll meet you here at two o'clock day after tomorrow if that's okay."

"Yes, that will give me enough time."

CHAPTER 39

The pictures she has given me are pretty good. There's one of four ladies including my customer. Their heads are close together. I might rearrange them a little, but this basic layout is what I'll use. There are also individual pictures of each lady. I guess by the way they're dressed that they are all well to do. My customer is the prettiest.

After studying the pictures for a while, I finally start putting paint on the tray. I use most of my white on the background. I'll have to get more paint if I'm going to be able to sell paintings. The layout on the tray is going to be larger than the group photo and I've decided to swap the positions of the middle two. The one with big hair and a larger face needs to be in the back. The one with a long nose has her hair parted in the middle. She's going to get a hairstyle that's a little bit different, and a very slight nose-job. I'm not going to change much, but the painting is going to look better than the pictures. I hope they won't mind.

While I'm waiting for the background to dry completely, I study the pictures some more. It's harder than when I painted my mom. I don't know these faces intimately.

Once I start painting, it's fun. I wish I had a pencil. I could use it to make light outlines and it would be easier to keep the right perspective. Instead, I paint all the mouths first. That establishes positions for the faces. I start on the left one.

By the time I decide it's time for a break, I've got the first face almost completed. I think it's looking good.

I cook some oatmeal in my pot and then make two slices of toast in the frying pan. Using my finger, I spread peanut butter on the toast and then use the toast slices to scoop oatmeal out of the pot. A spoon would be nice. I should make a shopping list, but I don't have a pencil.

It's late when I finally climb into bed. I should have quit a while ago because it's too dark in here now to paint, but I was having fun, and I hated to quit. I feel good about what I've accomplished. I'm lucky to have a room, too. I'm still scared, though. Mom is always in my thoughts when I go to sleep and tonight's no exception. Memories of when she was well come and bring sadness.

I was tired when I went to bed, but now sleep is avoiding me and all the strange sounds don't help. It sounds as if someone is dragging a chain across the floor and putting it in a pile I can't imagine what's happening.

Images of prison keep flashing across the screen of my mind. I wonder how Marie is doing. We weren't cellmates for very long, but we understood each other. She's just a kid. She should be part of a family, not in jail. Doreen was a friend too, but we never shared very much. Marie is my closest friend this side of New Mexico and I'll never see her again. I'll never see New Mexico again either. Even if I could get there, they'd find me in a heartbeat. I may never see Dad or my Grammy in Maine again either. They can't help me and I'm sure they're being watched anyway.

Trying to think positive thoughts usually helps, but not tonight. There is no one in this whole world that I could ask for help. Grammy Albert and Mom are both gone and there's no one else. The knowledge that I'm so completely alone crushes in on me like a live creature, sucking all the air from my claustrophobic little room. I put my clothes on and go outside to get out of the little room. I'm in a hurry. I don't even bother to put on a disguise. I walk down the street to get to a place where it's dark. There's no one to see me anyway. I almost start running, but I'm afraid that if I do, I won't be able to stop. I look up into the sky and try to pray, but there are a million stars between God and me. I don't think my prayers are getting through. After going back to my room, I crawl into bed. I always try to think of myself as tough, but tonight I have to slide my pillow over because the spot under my head is wet with tears.

CHAPTER 40

When I wake up, I'm lost again for a few seconds. The sun is turning the bricks of the building across the alley to gold, and my mood isn't as dark as it was last night, either. I may be all alone and on the run, but so far, I'm making it and I've even got a few dollars ahead. Eventually they're going to think that I've left the area and it will be easier to travel to another state or maybe even another country. In a way, it's good that I don't have any ties.

After more oatmeal and toast, I start painting again. Sunlight reflecting through the window helps a lot. I need lots of light when I'm selecting and mixing colors, and also when I'm painting fine details. After a few minutes I'm on autopilot. Everything except the painting is gone. I'm almost in a trance.

My watch says two-fifteen when I land on earth long enough to decide to take a break. My painting is really looking good. I think painting portraits may be my thing. Trying to make people's faces come alive with paint is fun and I think I'm good at it.

Thoughts of oatmeal again don't exactly turn me on. I think I'll go for a bike ride. Get a little exercise and buy a few things that I need. I hate to spend money, but tomorrow should be payday if the tray is finished. That shouldn't be a problem; it'll probably be finished by the time I go to bed.

I'm a boy again and after wheeling my bike out to the street, I head out of town and go for a good long ride. The sun's so bright that I need the sunglasses for more than just a disguise. I ride fast; I can feel my heart really

116

pumping. If North Carolina has her way, she'll try to stop it. On the way back to the dollar store, I hear violin music as I pass Mr. Ward's street. I still don't have him figured out.

While I'm at the dollar store I check out their jackknives and find one that's actually sharp. I need something to sharpen my pencils with and it's only a dollar. Along with pencils, I pick up a little package of silverware and a can-opener. Then while I walk down each isle to see if there's anything else that I can't do without, I spot light bulbs. I could use some more light, so I buy a package of two, hundred-watt ones. I select several cans of stuff to fight off starvation with, then head back to my room. For some reason, I'm not hungry after my bike ride. I take the lampshade off and swap the sixty-watt bulb for a hundred. With the lampshade removed, it won't get too hot. It's a lot brighter in here now. I forget about food and start right in painting again.

It's late when I eat a can of Spaghetti-O's and go to bed. I've got to start eating something that's healthy once in a while. It's hard without a refrigerator, or at least that's my excuse. When I have more money I'll do a better job shopping.

The painting is all done. I think it looks good and I'm anxious to find out what my customer thinks.

CHAPTER 41

This is going to be my lucky day. I don't know why, but I woke up feeling positive and that feeling is hanging on. The two eggs I fried were perfect and the toast was just right. With butter slathered all over everything and a fork to eat the eggs with, it's a good breakfast; although I do need a spatula. A flexible metal one, not one of those stiff ones that won't slide under an egg and definitely not one of those clubby plastic things that everything sticks to.

After breakfast, I turn myself into a boy, put my cap and sunglasses on, and take a bike ride out of the city. It's warm and sunny as I pedal through fields and woodlands as fast as I can. It occurs to me that I could ride my bike right out of North Carolina. Maybe I should just keep going. I'd need a map. I have no idea where this road goes. Besides, I need to know what the lady thinks of my painting, and it would be nice to have some more money.

When I come to a dirt road leading into the woods, I slow down and turn onto it. This is a mountain bike after all. I continue along slowly, hoping to see some animals. Selling paintings is going to require lots of new subjects, but the only animal I see is a woodchuck and when I try to get a better look at him, he disappears down his hole. After riding slowly on the dirt road for a few miles, I come to a paved highway. It probably goes back to the city, but I turn around and go back the way I came. A beautiful red cardinal is less skittish than the woodchuck. After I lay my bike in the grass beside the road, he lets me walk right under the little tree he's perched in. He has a pretty song and he's going to make a pretty painting.

When I get back to the mouth the dirt road, I resume my fast pace for a few more miles before turning back toward the city. By the time I get home, it's almost two o'clock. I've had a good workout. I take my bike inside, then go to the bathroom to clean up and change into my grannie outfit. I've got to be careful not to let one of the other tenants see me go into the bathroom as a boy and come out an old woman. I guess stranger things have happened, though.

CHAPTER 42

When I get to the violin man's alley it's exactly two o'clock and my customer is already here. I have the platter under my arm and I also have the envelope with the pictures.

"I can't wait to see it," she says as I approach.

"I hope you like it." I hand it to her along with the envelope of pictures, without making eye contact.

She studies the platter for what seems to be a couple of minutes. Her eyes move from face to face. She has no expression and I'm worried. Finally, she says one word.

"Marvelous!"

"I'm glad you like it."

"I love it. I should have had you do it on canvas. It's much too nice for a platter. Will you do another one for me?"

"Certainly, but wouldn't you rather have a portrait?"

"Yes, you're right. I would."

"How large would you like it to be?"

"Well, if I put it in the foyer, it should be about this big." She holds her hands about two feet apart.

"Okay, I can do that."

"In two days?"

"Maybe three for a portrait that big with lots of detail. I should have your pictures back to help my memory.

She hands me back the envelope.

"Don't take my picture out. Let's keep them all together."

"Do you want any changes in the hair style or

lipstick color?"

"I'll leave that up to you. I see you've changed Janice's hair a little. I like it. I'll bet she will too. How much do you want for the platter?"

She paid me thirty dollars for one of my squirrels. I expect she'll be generous.

"I'm sure whatever you want to pay me will be fair."

"How about if I give you a hundred dollars now and then we'll square up after you finish my portrait?"

"That would be fine."

"Good. I'll meet you here at two o'clock on Saturday."

"Could we meet somewhere else, maybe by the fountain? Mr. Ward has always had this spot by himself."

"Nonsense. Mr. Ward doesn't mind sharing this spot with you, do you Steve?"

"No Mrs. Gold."

"I didn't think so. In all the time I've been dropping money into Steve's hat, I've never known him to be unfriendly. By the way, my name's Amelia Gold." She extends her hand.

"Verna Kent."

I shake her hand. This is some scary.

"I'll see you here at two on Saturday." She walks off with the platter under her arm.

I'm shocked. Mrs. Gold. She's probably related to Donny Gold. Could even be his mother. I've got well over a hundred dollars now. I should get a map and ride my bike right out of this state now, today.

I should, but I don't. I hurry to change into a boy, then I ride my bike to Walmart and get a canvas and some more paint. I like painting portraits and I want to paint a big one of pretty Mrs. Gold. Stupid, but I'll just do this one last one, then I'm out of here. When I get home from Walmart, I don't even get something to eat before I start painting. I guess I must be getting hooked on painting people's faces. People's faces that I like, anyway.

CHAPTER 43

I finish painting Mrs. Gold on Friday morning. I can hardly wait for Saturday. I really like this portrait and I'm anxious to find out what she thinks of it. While I'm waiting, I ride to Walmart for another canvas and paint the cardinal I saw on my bike ride. When it's finished, I check to see if Mr. Ward is working. He is, so I change into grannie and take the cardinal over to his alley to sell.

When I get to the alley, Mr. Ward stops playing.

"If I make you nervous or something, I'll leave. I was going to try to sell this painting, but I don't have to. In fact, you can have it. Maybe you can sell it."

"No, you don't make me nervous. I'm sorry about the way I acted the other day. In fact, I was thinking that maybe you would go to dinner or a movie with me. My treat. I've been kind of lonely since my wife died. That's why I'm out here playing the violin."

"That's very nice of you to ask. Someone that I was very close to died just last week, and I don't think I'd be very good company yet. Thank you very much for asking me, though."

Wow. He asked me for a date. That's sad. I wonder what he'd think if he knew that I'm fifteen.

"If you feel like singing to any of my songs, I'd like it."

"Thank you. It just sort of happened. I don't even know most of the songs that you play."

I prop the painting of the cardinal against the wall and the first man that walks down the sidewalk stops and looks down at it. Before he can pick it up, Mr. Ward speaks up.

"I'll give you twenty five dollars for your painting."

"Thirty."

"I'm sorry. Mr. Ward has already bought it." The guy smiles at me, tips his hat and walks on.

When I get home, I have some lunch while I think about Mr. Ward. His change of attitude is amazing. Mrs. Gold's influence was part of it, I'm sure, but he seems to have really changed. I don't even know him, but I feel sorry for him. I wonder if I could get away with having dinner with him. Don't even think it. If I blow my cover, I'm sunk. Dealing with Mrs. Gold is already too risky. I try to flush Mr. Ward out of my mind then change into a boy and ride my bike over to a Salvation Army store to do some shopping. I need some different clothes.

"They're for my grandmother." I tell the clerk as she rings up my grannie clothes, although she doesn't ask or act suspicious. Besides the clothes, I buy a couple of used books and on the way home, I buy a newspaper. A little blurb on the front page says that I might have left the area. That's good. Maybe things will eventually calm down and I can really go someplace else.

CHAPTER 44

At one o'clock on Saturday, I finish reading one of my books. It was about a nurse in the First World War. It was really sad and I'm still teary over it. I fix some lunch and try to calm myself. I empathize with the characters in books way too much.

After I finish eating, I turn myself into grannie. I'm getting to be an expert. I'm finished reading the newspaper, so I decide to wrap the portrait in it, but before I do, I rub it with a towel to make sure the ink won't come off on my painting. I walk out the door and lock it.

I get to Mr. Ward's alley at exactly two o'clock. Mrs. Gold is already there and there are three other ladies with her. They don't look like the FBI and even though I'm kind of out of shape, I'd guess that I can outrun any of them, especially, since they all have high-heeled shoes on. Even so, I'm still scared, until I notice that they are the ladies that I painted on the platter. When I walk up, Mrs. Gold, Amelia, (I've got to start calling her that because I'm older than she is,) makes the introductions. She must be nice. She treats me like an equal although it's obvious that I'm nowhere near their social stratum. I just stand there. I feel kind of off balance with all these people looking at me.

"May I see the portrait?"

"Oh. Of course." I hand over the painting. I'd have been nervous even if there weren't a whole bunch of people, but that definitely makes it worse.

They briefly look at the painting.

"Do you mind if we discuss it in private?"

"Not at all. I'll meet you back here tomorrow if you want me to."

"That won't be necessary. Just give us a few minutes."

They all get into a big black Lincoln that's parked at the curb.

I walk over to listen to Mr. Ward.

"How about singing 'Danny Boy' again?"

"I don't know if I can. They are trying to decide if my painting is good enough, and I'm pretty nervous."

"I'm sure your painting is first rate. You can do it. Here we go." He starts playing and I sing.

"Oh Danny Boy…." People are stopping to listen. We make it to the third stanza before the ladies get out of the car…. "And I am dead as dead I well may be." I have tears in my eyes. Too much empathizing again. Mrs. Gold, Amelia, comes over to me.

"That was beautiful. You're very talented. Why haven't I heard of you?"

Oh you've heard of me alright. I just want to run.

"The girls all like what you've done. In fact Janice borrowed the platter and took it to her hairdresser and had him copy the style you gave her in your painting on the platter. After looking at my portrait, they've all decided they love it. They all want one too. We think that five hundred dollars apiece would be a fair price if that's acceptable to you. What do you think?"

"I think you're being more than fair. It will take me three days for each one, though, and I'll need some more pictures. I've seen you quite a few times, but I don't know these ladies. I should see each lady again to refresh my memory before I start painting her. Can I pick up the pictures tomorrow at two?"

"That would be fine."

After leaving them, I go back to my room and change into a boy, then I ride over to Walmart and buy some more canvases. The next afternoon, after picking up the pictures, I start painting Janice. I know I'm pushing my luck, but I can't seem to help myself.

CHAPTER 45

When I deliver Janice, all the ladies are there to meet me again. It makes me feel good that they all think the portrait is wonderful. I wanted to tell them that now that I know them a little better, I'd be able to do the last two in two days apiece, but I decide not to. I'm afraid the last two might feel slighted if I spend less time on theirs.

All the ladies are present again for the unveiling of the last portrait. They really like that one too, and again tell me what a great job I've done. Besides making lots of money, I've had fun. I'm sorry that it's over. Now I really do have to run. I hate to leave this routine that has begun to feel almost safe. I still carry all my cash with me all the time, though, just in case.

When I get ready to leave, the ladies all tell me again how happy they are with their paintings. I'm happy, with all the praise and all the money. The last thing that Amelia says to me, though, is that she'd like to meet me one last time tomorrow. I can't imagine what that's all about, but I'm suspicious and scared.

I worry about it all that evening. It's not just that Amelia might be going to turn me in. I've come to almost consider her to be a friend. I'm going to feel betrayed and rejected again if she does. I can't expect her not to though, considering the family ties with Todd Richardson.

I finally come up with a plan which I execute the next day. At one thirty, I ride my bike around the area checking things out. At one fifty-five, I ride past Mr. Ward's alley. Amelia is there already, but I don't see any FBI people. I hurry back home and quickly do the grannie thing, then rush back to meet her. I get there at two-ten. I've always been there at exactly two o'clock before.

"I'm sorry I'm late." I don't want to lie, so I don't offer an excuse.

"It's not a problem. You're not very late."

She gets right down to business.

"We've got a job for you if you're interested."

"What kind of job."

"We have a trucking business. We have lots of different kinds of trucks and we like to decorate them and keep them looking nice."

"I don't think I'd be very good at that. I've never painted anything very big."

"We have someone to do the painting. What we need is someone to paint the portrait of each driver on his door and I know you can do that."

"I'm kind of a recluse. I couldn't paint with people around."

"That would be perfect because you'd have to do it at night in the garage. There wouldn't be anyone else there."

"How would that work?"

"The garage closes at six. There would never be anyone in the building after that. We'd give you a key and you could do it any time you wanted. As long as you were gone before six in the morning, no one would even know you were there."

"How could I contact you?"

She gives me a key and a card with her phone number on it.

"There's a phone in the garage. I've already had pictures of the drivers taken. They'll be lying on the seats. You don't have to be as fussy as you were with us girls, but I would like them to look nice. The garage is at Number One Lynn Street. That's a good area and it's safe enough there. There will be some trucks that are ready to paint in the garage tonight. Just give it a try. If you decide not to do it, let me know."

Before I can even think about it, she gets in her car and drives off.

CHAPTER 46

I can't believe I'm even considering doing this. I should be out of here, now. Part of the reason that I'm going to try it is dumb. I don't want to disappoint Mrs. Gold...Amelia. I like her, but there's no way that I could ever be her friend, in fact, if she finds out who I am, she'll hate me. If she knew, I'm sure she'd turn me in in a heartbeat.

I turn into a boy, then treat myself to a meal that's as decent as you can get in a restaurant. At least, it has vegetables. A little convenience store has city maps and I'm soon pedaling toward Lynn Street. Stupid. I should have bought a state map and used it to ride out of here.

It doesn't take long to find the garage. It's a big brick building on the corner. It's almost too clean to be a garage. If it weren't for the four huge doors in the front, it could be mistaken for an office building. There's no one in sight and there are no cars in the parking lot. Everyone was supposed to leave at six, and apparently they did, but I've decided to wait until seven, so I ride around for a while

I pedal slowly around the area for a few minutes to kill time, then circle the block one last time to check things out before going to the door. I turn my bike around before lowering the kickstand. This could be a trap and I want to be able to get away fast if I have to. There's a doorbell, so I push the button just to make sure that there's no one inside.

"Hello."

I almost jump out of my skin. There's someone here. Then, before I can get on my bike, I hear the rest of the message.

"Our hours are six to six. If this is an emergency, call the number on the card beneath the phone."

I look up and sure enough, there's a phone.

There's a heavy lock on the door, but the key turns easily. Inside, several light switches are mounted on the wall beside the door. I flip one up and a row of lights down one side lights up. I hurriedly wheel my bike inside before closing and locking the door.

This is a big building and there are four trucks parked inside. I open the door of the closest one and there's a photograph lying on the seat, just like she said. It's not the guy who caught me in the back of his truck. I close the door again. I haven't decided to really do this yet.

The truck is nice and clean. I shouldn't have any trouble painting on the door. It's time to decide if I'm really going to do it. I look around. It's still pretty dark, so I flip more switches and light the place up. After wandering around, I find a relatively clean bathroom with a shower, a candy machine, and a soda machine. There's also a refrigerator. Heck, except for a bed, this place is better equipped than my room.

I know that I should forget this whole stupid idea and ride my bike right out of here. On the other hand, it would probably be easy to hitch a ride in one of these trucks and I might be able to take my bike with me. The doors of two of the trailers are unlocked. They are packed with bales of cotton. I'll bet those are going to be delivered someplace other than North Carolina. I could just sneak on board and I'd be out of here tomorrow. I might need food and water though, and how will I get out of the trailer? I decide to do at least one painting and plan my escape better.

I open the door of the truck that's closest to my bike again and this time, I study the photo that's lying on the seat. It's a bald man with glasses. I guess I'm really going to do it.

As I outline the guy's face on the door, I'm tempted to give him more hair and remove his glasses, but I don't. I want his customers to be able to recognize him. Right off, I decide that men are easier to paint. What you see is what you get. They don't wear makeup, and they probably aren't as fussy. There's lots of light and I finish this guy in about two hours. He looks pretty good too.

I paint another face and then start on the third one. This one's giving me some trouble. He's got some weird hairdo and I'm tempted to shave it all off. He'd be shocked when he saw it. I finally get it so that it looks good, or at least, it looks like the picture, but it took a lot of time. I'm not going to be able to do the fourth one. It's late when I head home. It's still dark, but it's starting to get light.

CHAPTER 47

The next morning, I stay in bed a lot longer than usual. That's not like me, but then I've never worked the night shift before. I don't feel very hungry, so I don't bother to eat anything. I turn into a boy and bike over to Walmart and buy a bike lock. After riding up to the jogging trail, I park my bike next to the other ones and lock it. It's a beautiful day and I really like this trail. I run hard for half an hour, then keep my pace as I run back. I feel good. I'm starting to get back in shape. I stop at a grocery store to get the makings for lunch. A steak, a potato, and some frozen mixed vegetables. I think Grammy spoiled me. I really like steak.

I'm hungry and even cut up the way Grammy did it, it takes a while for the potatoes to cook. If I had another hotplate, cooking would be a lot more convenient. I'd have to unplug my lamp though, and it would probably blow a fuse if I plugged two hotplates in at the same time anyway.

When everything is finally ready to eat, I gorge myself. It was worth the wait. When I'm finished stuffing myself, I take a nap, then read for a while. After my painting commitments, it feels good to have some time to just relax. When seven o'clock comes, I'm at an interesting place in my book, so I continue reading. I don't have a deadline, and if I wait until it's really dark, I won't have to worry about a disguise.

After I decide that it's dark enough, I ride over to Lynn Street without a disguise, except for my clothes and hat. There are too many lights though. I should have put my boy makeup on. Fortunately, there aren't many people around.

I'm nervous when I get to the garage. I feel like a thief sneaking around like this. There are cars driving by and I tell myself again how stupid I am to be doing this. I've already got lots of money. I'm doing this as a favor for Amelia more than anything. As soon as I get my bike inside and lock the door, I feel better until I turn on the lights.

The truck in front of me isn't an eighteen wheeler, or even a regular box truck. It's backed in and it's a big red tough-looking four wheel drive truck. Sinister, I'd call it. Even the grill looks menacing. On the body, over the cab, is the word "EXPLOSIVES" in large white letters. I walk around the evil-looking thing to check it out. It has a heavy steel body with padlocked doors. The lettering under the window on the driver's door reads:

"JACK'S DYNAMITE TRUCK"
"Don't Rock the Boat"

I'm afraid of it. I decide to check out the other trucks.

None of the ones I've already painted are still here. There's a truck backed into each of the four bays and I decide to start on the other end. The one farthest from the dynamite truck. I'll paint it last, if I have time. Amelia didn't tell me I'd have to paint on that thing. I guess Gold Trucking has about every kind of truck there is.

I'm getting pretty fast at painting these guys, but it's already later than the time I started last night. I'm going to have to hurry to get the dynamite truck painted before it starts to get light out. After I've painted the other three, I walk over to the big red monster and open the door, trying not to cause a vibration. The guy in the picture lying on the seat has dark curly hair. He's younger than the other drivers. He has a smile and nice eyes. He's kind of cute.

The key is in the switch in all these trucks and this one is no exception. The difference is that this truck has a little plastic encased picture on the key chain. To look at it, I have to climb into the seat, but I can't resist looking.

Heck, this truck isn't that different from our old Plymouth van. I could drive this thing. I pull the key out. The people in the little picture on the key chain are the curly-haired guy and a pretty girl. After studying it, I plug the key back in. There's also a larger picture of them taped to the dashboard. They look very young. She's showing off a diamond ring. They must have just gotten engaged. Her hair is every bit as black as his and she has beautiful laughing eyes. I'd love to paint them for a wedding present. So far I've put my V on quite a few portraits and I'd like to put it on one for them. What are you thinking? You don't have a life. You can't do things like that. I climb down from the cab and start painting.

Jack is starting to look pretty good, but there's something about his eyes in the picture in the cab that I'd like to capture. I climb back into the truck and study the picture taped to the dashboard for a few minutes.

As I start to climb back down from the cab, there's a noise by the door, the small one that I come through when I come to work. When I look up, the door opens and a man walks in. He just stands there looking at me; he's only about twenty feet away. I frantically look around, but I already know there's no way to escape.

"I saw you on the security camera. You're the girl

who murdered Todd. Don't even think about trying to get away. The police are outside."

"I didn't murder him it was self-defense. He was raping me and I didn't hit him that hard anyway. You're Mr. Gold aren't you? Ask Donny what happened. He was there."

Mr. Gold doesn't say anything. He just pushes a button on the wall. The big door in front of the dynamite truck opens, revealing a solid line of policemen. They all have big guns. I'm still hanging onto the hand hold beside the truck door, and I frantically climb back in.

CHAPTER 48

The dynamite truck starts instantly when I turn the key with the picture hanging on it. As I slam the door, I hear Mr. Gold shout.

"Don't shoot. That truck will explode."

I move the shifting lever to "D" and have to stretch to stomp the accelerator to the floor. Thank heavens it's an automatic. The cops try to rush me, but they're forced to scatter when I come roaring out through the big door. I narrowly miss my new high-tech bike. The streetlights help me get out through the gate and down the street. They also help me locate the light switch and the four-wheel drive lever.

This thing might be a big clunky old truck, but it can really go. I know that I'm going to see blue lights in the mirror very soon, but the cops haven't caught up with me yet.

I'm almost out of town before I see the police in the side mirror. Their blue lights are flashing, but they're just following me. They must be afraid of this dynamite truck. That's not very comforting, but it's working for now. I slow down and they keep their distance.

By the time I've traveled about twenty miles out of town it gets light enough for me to see a big power line crossing the highway. I guess it's time to find out what this thing will do. As I turn onto the power line right-of-way, I pull the four-wheel drive lever.

I'm not getting stuck, but I wonder how much bouncing around dynamite can stand. The cops can't follow me, so I slow way down.

Eventually, I come to a river that I know I can't

cross. By now it's pretty light and I can see a railroad trestle about a quarter of a mile down the river. I shut the truck off and push in the knob that turns off the lights. I don't have a plan, but I've lost my cover, my room, and my bike. I'm in real trouble. The cops will be swarming all over this whole area before long, and they'll have their dogs.

When I start walking down the river, I see plastic grocery bags that were left stuck in the bushes when the last flood receded. I stuff a bunch of them in my pockets as I head for the trestle. When I get to the railroad tracks, I stop and tie the plastic bags over my sneakers, then cross the tracks and continue on down the river. Hopefully, when the dogs lose my trail they'll think I walked on the rails.

My progress down the river is slow because I'm worried about snakes. As I start to come into a clearing, I hear dogs barking. I don't see how the police could have gotten here before me, so I continue on, slowly. The clearing turns out to be a trailer park on the bank of the river. Several dogs are chained-up. I don't think I can take the time to go around it, through the woods, so I hurry along in front of the line of trailers. It hasn't been light for very long, and I hope that everyone is still asleep in spite of the barking dogs.

About three quarters of the way across the park is a red Dodge Charger with the hood up. It even has a big 01 on the door and a Confederate flag on the roof. I'm hurrying past when someone calls out.

CHAPTER 49

"Where you goin in such a hurry, this time of day?"

The voice is coming from under the car, so he can't see me.

"Nashville. Can you give me a ride?"

"Couldn't take you to Nashville. Too far."

"I'd pay you."

"Too far. Might be able to get you to Knoxville."

"That would work if you could go right now."

"How much?"

"How much do you want?"

"Probably two with the price of gas and all."

"Too much. I'll give you one."

"Couldn't do it for less than one and a half."

"Done."

"In advance."

He slides out from under the Charger.

"Hey! You're the girl they're looking for."

"Five," I say.

"Done, but you have to buy me breakfast. Name's Billy, by the way."

"Verna."

I pay him then sit in the car. He messes with the engine for a minute, picks a can of beer off the fender, then slams the hood. He looks me over thoroughly while he climbs in beside me.

"Kind of early for beer isn't it?"

"It's never too early for beer."

This guy's probably about twenty. He looks like a hillbilly, but he thinks he's a race car driver. I don't trust him, but the sun's behind us, so I guess we're headed west. We stop at a little diner so he can go in and get us some breakfast.

"I want a coke in a glass bottle. I collect them. Get a half liter if you can. It doesn't have to be Coke, but it has to be a glass bottle."

I give him fifty dollars and don't expect any change. I sit in the car with my cap pulled down. It seems like he's been gone for a long time and I'm getting nervous. I keep watching up the road, ready to run if a cruiser comes around the corner. Finally he comes out with two real good breakfast sandwiches. He also has a couple of beers for himself and some kind of lemonade in a glass bottle for me. It's not Coke, but it'll do. I didn't realize I was hungry, but I am. The sandwich does the trick.

These roads are all really crooked. I guess he must know where he's going. I sure hope he does. I'll feel better about it when we hit I-40. He's not talking, just driving too fast, and after that ride with Grammy, I know what too fast feels like. When he does start talking, I wish he'd just concentrate on driving too fast.

"You know there's a big reward out for you. I could just drive you over to the police station. The other thing we could do is pull into one of these side roads and check to see if you really are a girl. In the paper, it said that you are Mexican, but you don't look like no wetback to me. Are you really a girl? You've got boy's clothes on and you look sort of like a boy. You don't have much for boobs. I'm just not sure."

"The other thing you could do is slow down a little and pay attention to your driving."

"Oh I'm pretty good at driving. I can probably check to see if you're a girl and drive at the same time."

"Do you know why there's a reward out for me?"

"You killed someone I guess."

"That's right. I killed a big football player with a glass bottle. Why do you think I wanted a glass bottle? Compared to him, you'd be a pushover. Please slow down."

Well, that ended his talk about checking me out, but it didn't do anything about his driving too fast.

"If we get caught for speeding, we're both going to be in trouble."

"Yeah. Especially you. I'd collect the reward."

He speeds up even more.

We've just passed a sign for the junction of I-40 and I know that we can't make it around the on ramp at this speed. He isn't slowing much. Somehow we drift around the ramp without hitting anything but when we get to the bottom, there's a state police cruiser waiting for us. I think Billy wants to get caught. He pulls right over behind the flashing blue light.

Before Billy can say who I am, the trooper has smelled the beer on his breath and is making him walk a straight line heel to toe in the ditch behind the car. I slide into the driving seat start the Charger and pull out around the state trooper's cruiser. This thing is really fast. I pull off at the next exit before the trooper catches up with me. I have to slow down on this road and when I look at the speedometer I notice that the gas gauge is on empty. The trooper still isn't behind me. He must not have taken the exit that I took.

When I come to a little town I stop at the gas pump. I don't have a credit card so I have to go inside to pay. I think the guy recognized me, but I get on the road as fast as I can.

It's almost noon so I keep the sun to my left as much

as I can. I think I'm going west and I should be coming to the Tennessee border before long. A faint thumping noise quickly gets louder. I hope it's a flat tire, but I don't think it is. I can see it now; it's a helicopter. I'm in real trouble. I can't outrun it and that confederate flag on the roof is a dead giveaway. I keep going hoping that I'll think of something. The sky is getting dark and although I wish that night would come I know it's many hours away.

When I get to a thick pine forest I pull over and stop. I shut off the engine and drop the keys on the floor board, then I climb out of the car and run into the forest. The helicopter circles overhead, but by staying under the trees I can hide from him. I work my way farther into the forest and then I let him see me. While he circles that area, I sneak back to the road keeping out of sight. When he has his back to me, I sprint across the road and dive into the ditch on the other side, hoping that I won't land on a snake. When the helicopter is back-to me again, I get up and run into the woods on this side of the road. I haven't gone very far before I hear a bunch of sirens. Trying to forget about snakes; I run through the woods as fast as I can while thorns tear at my clothes.

My first thought when I hear a loud explosion is that they are dropping bombs on me. When I feel a drop of rain on my face I realize that what I heard was thunder. When I hear the helicopter approaching, I flatten myself against the trunk of a thick pine tree. He flies directly over me then continues on until the sound of his rotor fades out completely. I guess he doesn't want to fly in a thunder shower.

I continue to hurry through the woods and suddenly come out on top of a steep rocky wall that falls away to a creek below. As I pick my way down to the creek it starts raining harder. I wade up the creek about fifty yards then cross it and climb part way up the opposite bank. I crouch under a rock overhang which protects me from the rain and gives me a clear view of my back trail. Although at first I'm worried about snakes, there don't seem to be any, and my little shelter is actually quite comfortable.

CHAPTER 50

I stay in my little protected spot all afternoon watching, but no one is following me. It must be raining hard enough to prevent the dogs from picking up my scent. All that rain on the road probably made it impossible for them to follow me. I think I'll stay here until dark, but then I'm going to have to move. In the morning this whole area is going to be swarming with police. Maybe before morning if the rain stops.

When it's almost dark, I crawl out into a downpour. I'm glad it's warm. I wade back across the creek, then angle up toward the road. Before I get there I begin to think that I'm lost. I keep going, but I'm worried that I might be going in the wrong direction. Continuing to go through the woods isn't going to work. They'll eventually find my trail, and the dogs will follow me. I've got to get back to the road. With all this rain they'll never be able to track me there. I was getting discouraged, but I can occasionally hear a car now, so I know I'm going in the right direction. I went into the woods a lot farther than I thought I did.

When I get back to the road it's very dark and it's still raining hard. The water dripping off my nose tickles. Back down the road, I can just make out the interior light of a police cruiser. I came out close to where I went into the woods. I wasn't off course very much. I know the cop sitting nice and dry in his cruiser down the road can't see me. I turn and start slowly running up the edge of the road. This is going to be a long run and I want to go just fast enough to keep warm, but slow enough to be able to run all night. An occasional flash of lightning momentarily illuminates the roadway. Many of the trees beside the road have had their branches trimmed to keep them from touching the power lines and the lightning flashes makes them look naked as they pull back from the road. They seem to be trying to avoid the high-voltage wires.

About a mile up the road the sound of an approaching car tells me to get off the road. I step into the ditch and hunker down so his lights won't find me. When he passes water sprays everywhere. I run a little faster for a while to warm up again.

About five miles up the road, I run into a problem. Streetlights. There are only three of them; it's not much of a town, but to avoid running in the light where someone might see me, I have to sneak behind buildings. A dog barks and I'm afraid he might come after me, but he doesn't. Probably this heavy rain discourages him. He's got more brains than I have.

A few more little towns cause me problems, but even so, I'll bet I've traveled close to fifty miles by the time there's just a hint that it might start to get light. I haven't seen a "Welcome to Tennessee" sign though. It's too early and raining too hard to tell where the sun is going to come up. I must not be going in the right direction. I wouldn't be safe in Tennessee either, but the police there probably wouldn't be as determined to catch me.

It's starting to get just a little bit lighter now, and it's still raining hard. Even though I'm still running slowly, I'm cold. I'm out of energy. I'm in trouble again. Through the gloom, another tiny town emerges. Just before I get to it, I cross a little bridge. The water flowing beneath it looks as cold as I feel. My brain isn't working very well, and before I realize what I'm doing, I've run right through town. I don't see any place that I could crawl into to get out of the cold rain. Just one little store, and a few houses. I was lucky, apparently no one saw me. I just keep going.

Just the other side of town, I come to a dirt side road with a bunch of mailboxes at the end of it. My cold foggy brain comes up with an idea. There are no phone lines going down the road and since this is hilly country, I doubt that cellphones will work here. These people won't be able to call the police very fast. Maybe I can find a place to get out of the rain and get some sleep. I start down the dirt road at a pretty slow pace for me. I don't have the energy left to run fast enough to warm up. I'm cold.

CHAPTER 51

Not far from the mouth of the dirt road that I'm on is a bridge. It's just a one-lane wooden bridge. There can't be much traffic on this road. Beyond the bridge, the dirt road is only about a half-mile long. It's hard packed so I'm not getting my running shoes muddy. The road ends at a clearing on a small lake with cottages lined up along the near shore. It's still not very light out, and in this rain, I can barely make out the far shore. I only see one cottage over there. Most of the cottages on this side appear to be empty, but three of them have a car or pickup truck parked in front. The cottage that is farthest away doesn't have a car in the yard, but it has what looks like a small barn behind it.

I skirt the clearing, keeping just inside the woods, and come out behind the barn. It has a padlock, but isn't locked. Once I'm inside, I discover that instead of a barn, it seems to really be a combination woodshed and storage shed. In the dim light coming through the one dirty window, I look around for something to cover up with. There are a lot of things that I'd classify as junk, but I luck out. I find a tote with dry bedding in it. I'm shivering violently as I unroll a piece of carpet and spread some thick quilts on it. After stripping to my underwear and draping my wet clothes over an old chair, I climb between the quilts and pass out.

When I wake it's completely dark. It's a lot safer to travel in the dark. I've got to get going before the sun comes up, but I'm warm and dry. I'll get up and put those cold wet clothes on in just a minute. I try to think what my next move should be, but I'm asleep again before I can think at all.

When I wake again, I've missed my chance to travel in the dark. The sun is shining through the window. It's also shining on the outside of the barn wall that I've been sleeping next to and heat is radiating from it. I've slept too long, but at least I'm warm and rested. When I put my clothes on, they're still wet, but they don't feel very cold. I put everything back the way I found it, then peek out the door. Two camps back up the pond, an old Ford truck is parked by the driveway. There's another pickup in the driveway and I think the Ford might have a "For Sale" sign on it. As I watch, an old man walks around the side of the cottage and starts trimming a bush. Probably a rosebush. I walk out of the barn and quietly close the door behind me. I can tell now, from this angle, that the old truck *does* have a "For Sale" sign on it. It would be the ideal way to get out of the area and finally make it to Tennessee.

"Does your truck run okay?"

"Yes, it runs. How'd you get here?"

A curtain just moved inside the cottage. That makes me nervous.

"I've been walking, but it would be a lot quicker if I had a truck. What are you asking for it?"

"It's really my grandson's, but I think he's asking five-hundred for it. Where'd you come from?"

"We just moved up here from Albuquerque. Has it got any gas in it?"

"Probably not much. How far you goin?"

"Not too far, but I don't know the area. I don't want to run out of gas."

"I've got some in a five gallon can in the garage, if you're interested. Are you old enough to drive? That

149

truck's a standard shift."

"I've been driving for two years. I learned in a standard. If you throw in the gas, I'll give you three for it if it'll run."

"Can't do that. My grandson'd shoot me. Four."

"You won't get many buyers down here. Three-fifty."

Getting the gas from the garage seems to take him forever and I'm getting nervous. While he's dumping the gas in, I look over my shoulder. There's a cellphone tower on the hill across the lake. I could be in trouble again. I quickly pay him and climb into the truck. It's hot inside, so I roll the window down. It starts right up and I drive back up the dirt road faster than I should. I have a bad feeling, that I've been reported.

I've crossed the bridge, and I'm almost back to the highway. What looks like a woods road branches to the right. Must be the access to the cellphone tower, or the other side of the lake. I'm afraid there might be cops waiting at the end of this road, so I decide to take the turn, or at least check to see if it's passable. The brakes on the Ford aren't much, and I'm past the woods road before I can stop. I'm having trouble getting the truck into reverse. It just won't go. After a few unsuccessful tries, I just jam it in. I'm in a hurry, and I stall the engine. Through the open window, I hear a familiar sound before I can try to get the engine started again. A police radio. They *are* waiting for me at the highway.

I try to shift to neutral so that I can start the engine. No luck. It's now stuck in reverse. Pushing the clutch in doesn't work either. When I try to start the engine, the starter moves the truck backward. I push the clutch in as hard as I can, but it still doesn't disengage. Finally, I decide to abandon the truck. I turn the key to start and let the starter crank the truck backwards into the mouth of the woods road. I cut the wheel so that it ends up crosswise. That should stop them from following me in their cruisers, and I'm pretty sure that I can outrun them on foot. I jump out of the truck and lock the doors. I shove the key into my pocket, and run.

CHAPTER 52

I'm running as if my life depends on it. It does. I know those cops will have guns. Half a mile up the woods road is a fork. I guess the left one goes to the cell tower, and the right one goes to the back side of the lake. I know the cops are close behind me. I don't have time to think about my choice. The cell tower is on a steep hill. With the truck stuck across the road, the cops will have to chase me on foot, and I'm banking on them being out of shape. I take the left fork and start up the hill.

The road ends at the cell tower. I don't know where I am, so I climb a little way up the tower. I can see the whole countryside, including the road that I just ran up. It looks like five cops following me. They are still almost half a mile away, but they all have long guns. I don't know how close they have to be to shoot me. I'd better get down from this tower. If I can see them, they can see me. Just then, the cop who is in the lead, stops. A little puff of smoke comes from his gun. A bullet ricochets from a rock on the hillside below me and then the sound of a shot echoes across the valley. I'm only about ten feet up the tower, and I just grab a bar down near my feet, and drop the rest of the way down.

The closest thing that I could see from the tower was the lake. It looked to be just down over the hill. They know I'm up here, so I look at where the sun is, and head straight to the lake. I didn't see any dogs, but if these cops don't have any, they'll get some in a hurry.

The lake is close, and it doesn't take me long to get to it. I know that I need to get in and swim to throw the dogs off my trail, but I hesitate. I don't know what creatures are living in this lake. One thing I do know, though, is that whatever creatures live here, they don't have guns. The bottom is muddy and slimy as I wade out far enough to start swimming. I'm a long way off, but the people across the lake, where I bought the truck, might possibly see me. Although it's hard with my clothes and sneakers on, I go slow and try not to splash water. I don't think the cops could hear me but just to be sure, I also try not to make any noise as I head back down the lake. I swim toward the end where the truck is stranded. I hope they'll think I went in the other direction. I'm seeing quite a few turtles, but so far, no snakes or alligators. I know there have to be some in here though.

The end of the lake that I'm heading toward is where the bridge is. When I crossed it. I noticed that the water was flowing to my left. It's the outlet for the lake. My plan, right now, is to hide under that bridge until dark. It's still morning, so I'm going to have a long wait, and the cops are going to have a long time to find me. If I walk down the outlet in the water the dogs won't be able to find my trail. They might smell me if I hide under the bridge, but I walked over that bridge last night. That might confuse them, although it was raining, and that might have washed away most of the scent. It's not a perfect plan, but it's all I've got right now.

CHAPTER 53

When I get to the outlet, it's wide and too shallow to swim. I either have to drag myself over the slippery rocks, or stand up. I don't dare to expose myself by standing up, so I slide my body over the slimy rocks, aided by the current.

In a few minutes I see the bridge and it's a scary sight. There isn't a very big opening under it for the water to flow, and it looks like the perfect place for snakes to hide. I'm tempted to just walk up over it and continue downstream. If I do, the dogs will pick up my trail on the bridge, and the cops will know where I've gone. I've got no choice. I've got to stay in the water and at least crawl through that claustrophobic, potentially snake infested little tunnel.

I'm only about a foot from the bridge, but I can't seem to force myself to slide into that dark little hole under it. The rumble coming from the direction of the highway is getting louder. A car is coming. I lie down flat and let the current sluice me under the bridge. I reach up and hang onto one of the timbers to keep from sliding farther underneath.

It's just a wooden bridge with planked-over timbers spanning the outlet from the lake. Cracks between the planks let light filter through. Once I'm underneath it, I can see fairly well. I'm still afraid that there might be snakes under here, but it isn't as claustrophobic as I thought it would be.

The car that's approaching suddenly stops. I think they must have seen me, but I don't know how. I hear doors open, then voices.

"Look at the size of that thing. It just crawled up from between a couple of those planks on the bridge. It's got to be ten feet long."

Running footsteps approach, followed by an extremely loud crash.

"What'd you do that for?"

"He was probably going to attack. I ain't takin no chances on a snake that big. He's got to be poisonous. I'll bet there's a whole nest of em under that bridge."

"He's not poisonous. That's a rat snake. They eat other snakes. You didn't get him anyway. I think he went into the water."

Great! Now I'm more worried than ever. I didn't see him; I wonder where he went. I guess I must have scared him out from under here, so maybe he won't come back.

I hear some stomping on the bridge and dust filters down through the cracks between the planks. Next, I hear one of the guy's portable radios.

"Did you get her?"

"No. Jake shot at a big snake. He thought it looked as if it were going to attack."

"Well stop shooting. She can tell where you are. You're supposed to try to take her alive if you can, you know."

"10-4."

"It wasn't going to attack us."
"You don't know that."

"Let's go check out this side of the lake like we're supposed to. It's not a very big lake. They'll be coming with the dogs in a few minutes if nobody finds anything. I think she went back toward the road."

The car doors slam and they drive over the bridge. After a few seconds, the sound fades. They're gone. Now what am I going to do? I'm afraid that there might still be snakes under here. I don't see any, but that doesn't mean there aren't any. I'm scared. Over to my left is kind of a shelf. The water must have washed the gravel away during a flood. I check it out carefully and don't see any snakes. I'm cold after being in the water for so long, and when I climb onto the ledge, I find that it has been warmed by the sun shining on the planks above it. Maybe I *could* stay here until it gets dark. Dark's a long way off, though, and I'm dying of thirst. I'm tempted to drink some of this scummy water, but I'm resisting. I stretch out to get more comfortable, if that's even possible when you're thirsty, dirty, and scared.

I see movement at the other end of the bridge. Across the little creek, a big snake raises his head up. I can't tell how long he is, but he's at least as big around as my arm. He's staying perfectly still, but he's looking right at me. He looks like he's ready to strike, although I'm much too far away. I wonder how many more of them there are under here. I don't think I can stay here. New Mexico probably has more kinds of snakes than North Carolina, but I don't know much about them. They've never been among my favorite creatures. Let's face it, I'm scared to death of them.

The big snake slides into the water and starts swimming directly toward me. He's really fast and he still has his head up. He almost reaches me before I come out of my trance of terror. I grab a handful of gravel and hurl it at his head. He stops and I give him another blast. He turns and slowly swims upstream, toward the lake. I immediately slide off my little shelf and let the current take me out from under the bridge.

I hurry down the creek, letting the current help while I watch for more snakes. I don't get very far before I come to a bridge over the highway. I remember this one from last night. It's next to a little town. This bridge is bigger, not so claustrophobic, but it's also a lot wider. After the last bridge, I can't make myself go under it. I decide to take my chances and run over the top of the bridge and get into the creek on the other side. I shouldn't leave much scent on the highway. My shoes are pretty well washed off from all the swimming and wading.

When I get up on the highway, I see something that causes me to make a snap decision. In front of the little store in town is a delivery truck. Red and white. It says "COKE" on the side. The driver is wheeling a dolly loaded with cases of soda toward the back of the store. When he disappears behind the store, I sprint to the truck.

There isn't much to hide behind in the back of the truck. There's a little space between the top of the cases of soda and the ceiling of the truck body, but I'm not sure that there's room for me up there. Even if there is I don't know how I'd get up there. I move a few cases of soda and try to make a place. Whistling "Oh Susannah," the delivery man comes back to the truck before I'm ready. I hide as much as I can, but I prepare to run and jump off the back of the truck if he sees me. He's studying something, paperwork I guess, as he shoves his dolly into the truck and slams the door and latches it. The truck starts and we're moving. Away from the cops.

It's dark in here, but I know that one of the cases that I moved was Sprite. That will work for me. Right now, I could drink almost anything that was wet. The second can takes me a little longer than the first one did. After I've drunk all the Sprite I can hold, I try to find a way to climb to the top of the soda cases in the dark. By climbing up the frame inside the body, while jamming my feet between the cases of soda, I manage to get up there. I don't know how I'm going to get down in a hurry and I'm not sure I'm hidden very well. I don't have a very long wait to find out. The truck is slowing down.

When the guy opens the door and light shines in, I'm temporarily blinded. I'm not hidden at all. He's staring right at my face. He slams the door shut again and latches it. I start crying. I'm caught. There's no way out of here. The delivery guy is going to collect the reward money. I climb down and bang on the door, but I don't hear anything for a long time. All the while, I hopelessly explore the dark interior of the truck body with my fingers. I try kicking on the door then I find the handles of the dolly the driver has put in the back of the truck. I repeatedly slam it into the door, but nothing works. The next sound I hear is sirens, lots of sirens.

Someone unlatches the door on the back of the truck, swings it open and jumps back. The light is so bright that for a few seconds, I can't see anything. I don't know if they think I'm some ferocious animal, or an alien creature. There are five cops lined up behind the Coke truck. One of them motions for me to get out of the truck. I sit down on the back edge of the truck body, and slide to the ground with my hands up.

The cops all walk up to me with their guns drawn.

Vicky's Escape

They'd love to have an excuse to shoot me. I think if I so much as blink one of them will do it, and his buddies won't tell. They handcuff my wrists and my ankles too while their guns are pointed at my face. After they're sure that I'm completely immobilized, they roughly pat me down and stuff me into the back of a cruiser. That quick, my life is over. All that time and effort I spent running was wasted. I just sit, tightly seat belted to the back seat of the cruiser, and cry.

CHAPTER 54

There are two state troopers in the car they put me in, and it has a heavy wire grate between the front and back seats. Not only do I have two sets of handcuffs on, the seatbelt is so tight that I can hardly move. All I can do is think and there isn't much that's positive to think about. It's a long ride, and after I am done crying and feeling sorry for myself, I think about what really happened the day I hit Todd.

School gets out at 3 o'clock but I had a meeting with Mr. Nelson that probably lasted 10 minutes. I ran pretty fast on the way home. I've run four miles in under twenty-seven minutes, but I was pacing myself because I was so wound up. I probably got to the Navigator by no later than three-forty. Although it seemed much longer, the encounter with the boys couldn't have taken more than about five or six minutes, so they should have easily had Todd in the hospital by four-thirty. I wonder what time he was actually admitted. Maybe they waited for him to get better so that nothing would be said and they wouldn't be accused of rape. That's not much, but it should be checked out. I wonder if I'll get Darrell for my lawyer again.

When I get to jail, everyone acts mad at me. They take my clothes, my money, my jack knife, the card with Mrs. Gold's phone number, the key to Gold's garage, the key to the old Ford pickup, and my room key. I fight with them about the necklace that Grammy gave me, and they temporarily let me keep it. I have to take a shower and put on a prison uniform. I don't have Marie for a cellmate this time around; in fact I don't have a cellmate.

Vicky's Escape

I'm in solitary.

I just sit on my bunk in a stupor. After all I went through to escape and avoid getting caught, I'm right back in here. I'm worse off than before. When the guard comes to slide my supper tray through the hole in the door I ask if I can make a phone call.

"Not while you are in solitary, but you can petition the warden."

"How do I do that?"

"I'll bring you a form."

It must be about a week later when the guards come. I'm not keeping track of time anymore, in fact, I'm not doing much of anything. I can do push-ups, sit-ups, and run in place, but that's about all. The two guards come into my cell and quickly lock the door behind themselves. They put handcuffs on me, then some leg irons with a chain between them so I can sort of walk. They lead me out of my cell and down the hall. I don't know if I'm going to the firing squad or what. Instead we end up in the warden's office.

"Why do you still have a necklace?"

"My Grammy gave it to me and before she died, I promised never to take it off. What harm can it do to honor an old lady's wishes?"

"How would I know that your grandmother gave it to you? It looks expensive. Did you steal it?"

"Read the inscription on the back."

My hands are handcuffed behind my back, so the warden gets up and walks around his desk. He turns the necklace around so that he can read it.

"Who's Gram A?"

"Grammy Albert. She was killed in an accident."

"You're her granddaughter?"

"Sort of."

He drops the necklace.

"Why should we allow you to make a phone call?"

"I thought you were always allowed to make a phone call."

"You *were* allowed to make one the first time you were here."

"Well aren't there some new charges or something?"

"I guess there will be, a lot of new charges. Maybe you should be allowed another phone call. Whom do you want to call?"

"Mrs. Gold. The mother of one of the boys."

"Why do you want to call her?"

"Because I like her; I consider her a friend, and I want her to know what happened."

"I think she already knows what happened."

"No she doesn't and neither do you. Those two boys and I are the only ones who know."

"I'll call her and see if she wants to talk to you."

"Her phone number is on a little card that they took from me when I got here."

"How did you escape?"

"I just went out the bathroom window at the courthouse and ran off."

"There must be more to it than that. Why couldn't they find you?"

"I don't know. I guess they didn't look in the right place."

"You had about $1300 when they caught you. We know you bought a truck and that you gave the guy with the red Dodge five-hundred dollars. Where did you get all that money?"

"Painting."

"You mean you worked as a painter for all that time and nobody recognized you?"

"I guess not."

"Unbelievable. I know you people are hard workers but that seems impossible."

"What do you mean you people?"

"Mexicans, Latinos, whatever. I know you don't look it, but everyone knows it's true. Especially with your accent."

"I'm an American. Not that I'm real proud of it right now. My dad is a citizen, and so am I."

"That may be but we can't change who we are can we?"

"Can I still have Darrell for my lawyer?"

"You will get whomever they appoint. Take her back."

A week later the guard gives me the message that Mrs. Gold doesn't want to talk to me.

CHAPTER 55

Darrell shows up a few days after my message from Mrs. Gold. He has to talk to me through the hole in the door.

"Well, we meet again."

"I tried not to come back but they thought I should. I asked for you but the warden told me that I didn't have a choice. They'd assigned a lawyer to me."

"I requested your case."

That's loyalty. He requested my case even though he knows I'm a loser.

"I thought maybe no one else would take my case. Thank you for believing in me."

"Well, maybe I shouldn't. Escaping sure didn't help us any. By the way, I've already made a motion for change of venue and the judge turned me down. I think he's really mad about your escape. You sort of made fools of the local law enforcement, not to mention the FBI."

"Well, I should be sorry about that, but I'm not. I was pretty sure that escaping was the only chance I had."

"It's been a while since I talked to you. Let's go over what happened again to refresh my memory."

"Okay."

I go over the whole day again trying to include even the smallest details that might be significant. I have to go slow because he's taking lots of notes while I'm talking.

"Can you think of anything at all that might be helpful or explain why they're sticking to a lie even though it might ruin your life?"

"I did think of one thing that might be important. When I looked back after running a little way, the other two boys were helping Todd into the car. He certainly wasn't dead at that point. He looked drunk, though. I went over the times and I think that they should have gotten him to the hospital by four thirty. I wonder when they actually did check him in. Maybe they thought that he was going to get better and if he didn't go to the hospital there wouldn't be an investigation or any accusations of rape. Maybe if they had gotten him to the hospital sooner he might have survived."

"Well I can certainly check to see when he was admitted."

"Good."

"I've been trying to get you out of solitary but so far no luck."

The guard tells Darrell that his time is up. He has to go.

"Thank you for coming."

"You're welcome. I'll be back."

I'm alone again.

The next day I get a phone call. They pass me the phone through the hole in the door. I think it must be my lawyer. Darrell's the only one who would be calling me.

"Hello."

"I don't know why I'm calling you."

It's Mrs. Gold.

"Hello Mrs. Gold. It's really good to hear your voice."

She ignores my comment.

"The warden said that you consider me a friend. I don't know how that could be; I certainly don't consider you a friend."

"I can understand that. I know that Todd was a friend of your family and especially Donny, but I didn't murder him. The last time I saw him he was alive. I did hit him because he was raping me. I just wanted to get him off me."

"He was raping you."

"Well, he had my pants down around my ankles and he was on top of me. I was terrified and I hit him."

"You think that I should believe you when my son is telling me a completely different story?"

"I know that you have to be loyal to your son, but I think that if you have a good long talk with Donny you might change your mind. He and Jason are the only two who know what really happened, besides me. You're the closest thing to a friend that I have. My mother died the same day as Todd and the Grammy that I loved has died since. We just moved here and everyone hates me. I can't get a fair trial here and if they convict me it's either life in prison or death."

"Goodbye."

She hangs up and I pass the phone back to the guard. I feel so awful and alone that I sit on my bunk and cry.

CHAPTER 56

I've lost track of time but I eventually get another phone call. This time it's Darrell.

"How are you doing?"

"I'm surviving."

"Are they letting you out at all?"

"No. Are you making any headway on getting me out of solitary?"

"Not yet, but I think they'll have to at least let you out for an hour a day. I'll keep working on it."

"Thanks. I appreciate your help."

"I checked on when Todd was admitted to the hospital. It was 7 o'clock but they have an excuse."

"What could they possibly have as an excuse for waiting so long?"

"They say he went to sleep and they didn't realize he was really in bad shape until they tried to wake him up. When he wouldn't wake up they rushed him to the hospital."

"That's stupid. Everyone knows that you don't let someone with a head injury go to sleep before you determine that they're okay."

"Well sometimes stupidity is a good enough excuse in court."

"What else is new?"

"Your trial is scheduled to begin a week from Thursday."

"I don't even know what day it is but I guess it doesn't make any difference. What about the probable cause hearing?"

"There isn't going to be one. The fact that you

167

escaped is probable cause enough. There *is* going to be an arraignment, though."

"What's that?"

"That's when the judge reads the charges against you, which now include escaping, avoiding arrest, and a bunch of other things. Like trying to run over cops. You get to plead innocent, or guilty. Or, you can just not say anything. That's usually if you're guilty, but you don't want it on your record that you admitted it."

"I didn't try to run over cops. They wouldn't get out of the way."

"Doesn't matter."

"When will the arraignment be?"

"I'm not sure yet. Probably in a couple of days. Before the trial, anyway. I could enter a waiver of arraignment. That way, we wouldn't have to go to the courthouse just to plead."

"At this point, I'm for doing anything that will get me out of this little hole, even if it's just for an hour or two."

"Okay. The state police will pick you up in the next few days and I'll meet you there."

"Isn't scheduling the trial for next week pretty fast?"

"Yes it is, but there's some pressure to hurry things along. We shouldn't complain though. There are prisoners in North Carolina who have been in solitary for over ten years."

"I'm pretty sure that I couldn't live that long in here."

"Well don't get discouraged. Your trial will take some time. This is just some of the preliminary stuff. I'm already doing the paperwork for an appeal."

"Sounds like you don't have much hope for a not

guilty verdict. Don't they have to convince everyone on the jury that there's no doubt that I'm guilty? I thought that if even one person had doubts they couldn't convict me."

"That's true and you can't tell what a jury will do, but we have to be prepared. We're in it for the long haul."

"What else is new? I suppose everyone is happy that I'm back in jail and not out terrorizing the whole world."

"Well, the mayor sure is. He had a special news conference where he bragged up the police force for their great detective work and bravery in your capture."

"Figures. The police had nothing to do with it. It was a Coke delivery guy who caught me."

"I didn't hear that, but there's been lots of publicity. Your father found out that you had some money and he tried to attach it. They wouldn't give it to him though, it's evidence."

"I guess he can't visit me because I'm in solitary."

"No, he can't."

Through the hole in the door, I can see the guard walk up behind Darrell and tell him that his time is up.

"Thank you for coming."

I'm alone again.

CHAPTER 57

Sure enough, a couple of days after Darrell's visit, the state police arrive. Two of them. They're big and in a sour mood. I guess they didn't like being outsmarted by a fifteen year old girl.

They handcuff my wrists behind the back and hook a chain between the ankles like the guards did when they took me to see the warden. I don't have a little female for an escort this time. With a big male state cop hanging on each arm, I finally get to leave my little hole. Home sweet home. I won't be gone for long enough though.

Before my escorts climb into the front seats of their cruiser, they roughly stuff me in the back, where there's already another bruiser to share the back seat with me. He looks so ugly that I'm tempted to snarl at him. I wonder if he'd hit me if I did. He must think that I'm a terrible low-life person.

I think of Grammy. She was wonderful and I really miss her. I'd like to feel my necklace, but my hands are behind my back. Not the most comfortable ride I've ever had.

This time I don't care what the courthouse looks like. I'm already pretty familiar with it, especially the roof. Not that it will do me any good. I'll never see that roof again. I don't want to either.

There are people standing on the sidewalk as my cops drag me up the front steps. Some of them are cheering. I've got a fan club. Once inside I'm pushed into the old elevator which eventually creaks and groans its way up to the fourth floor. I'm allowed to walk down the hall, and then one of the cops actually takes my handcuffs off before pushing me onto the seat beside Darrell.

"How are you going to plead?" he asks me quietly.

"Are you kidding? You know I'm not guilty."

"They might go easier on you if you plead guilty."

"You mean life in that little hole instead of death? No thanks."

The judge reads all the charges. The one I like best is, "attempting to run over ten police officers with a dynamite truck."

"How do you plead?"

"Not guilty."

"Not guilty, your Honor." The judge is a stickler for formality.

"Whatever."

"You could be charged with contempt, young lady."

"Are you going to kill me twice?"

"Get her out of here."

CHAPTER 58

Doing the kind of exercises that you can do in a six by eight jail cell without hitting the bunk or banging my leg on the toilet is pretty boring, but I've got to try to stay in shape as best I can. The days are going so slowly that I don't even try to keep track of them. Except for the meal trays being pushed through the hole in the door once in a while, I wouldn't know if it were day or night. I do know that my trial is coming up in a few days, but I don't know when.

I've just finished a set of a hundred pushups and I'm breathing hard when the guard tells me that I have a call from a lawyer. Those are the only calls that I'm allowed in here.

"Hello Darrell."

"I'm not Darrell. This is Attorney Ames."

"I'm sorry. I thought you were Darrell Jones."

"Oh, yes. He's a public defender."

"Yes, that's right. He's my lawyer."

"Yeah, well good luck. Anyway, are you really the Victoria Trent that Mrs. Albert mentioned to me?"

"Yes, I expect I am."

"Can you prove it?"

Already, I don't like this guy's attitude. Talking to anyone else is better than talking to myself, though.

"I don't know why I'd have to, but yes, I can prove it."

I reach inside my shirt and hold my necklace.

"When she died, Grammy was wearing a necklace that's identical to the one I have around my neck right now. They were custom made for her by a guy named

Stanley, from Wilmington. On the back of mine, it says "Vicky love Gram A." That should be pretty good proof."

"Well, we have to be sure. I remember that she changed her will before she died in an automobile accident, but at the time, my secretary handled the details and I didn't get very involved. I've just been going over her new will, and you're mentioned in it."

"I don't know why I would be. I called her Grammy, but I'm not really related to her at all."

"No, you aren't. In fact, she had no living relatives, which makes my job easier because nothing is being contested. Anyway, there's going to be a reading of her will a month from tomorrow and your presence is required."

"Well, I don't think that's going to work. I may very well be dead a month from tomorrow. If I'm not, I'll certainly still be where I am right now. In this jail, in solitary."

"Well you'll at least have to arrange to be represented at the reading."

"Mrs. Albert said that she'd talk to you about my defense."

"Yes she did, but like I told her, it would be a conflict of interest. I knew Todd Richardson and his family, and I represent Gold Trucking as their attorney. I don't do criminal law anyway, but if your lawyer can arrange for bail, we might be able to help with that."

"There's no chance of my getting out on bail. They won't even let me out of solitary."

"Sorry to hear that. Has Darrell already made a motion for change of venue?"

"Yes, but the judge turned him down."

"My office will notify you again a few days before the reading. Goodbye."

Even Grammy's lawyer is against me. Why would I be mentioned in her will? I'll probably never know. I wish I could hug Grammy right now.

CHAPTER 59

I thought that Darrell would at least call me again before the trial started, but he hasn't. It's too late now. The police are here to escort me to the courthouse again. I know that he's really busy. He probably has a chance of winning some of his other cases.

I get the handcuffs behind the back and chain between the ankles treatment again before the guard dares to open the door completely and stand aside. I have the same big ugly-looking cops for escorts that I had last time for the arraignment. They don't look as if they've sweetened up any. It's plain that they think that I murdered their star football player in cold blood. Maybe they think that they're in danger. That's a laugh, but I'll bet it wouldn't take much of an excuse for them to Taser me, or at least Mace me. I don't think they could get away with shooting me while I'm in handcuffs.

There's already a big guy in the back seat, just like before. When they stuff me in beside him he looks at me like I'm a piece of dirt. I can't imagine what kind of a person he must think I am. Maybe he believed the tabloid article that said I'm controlled by an alien being.

At depressing times like this, I always think of Grammy and say a little prayer for her. I think of how shocked I was when she gave me my necklace. I wonder what will happen to it if they execute me. I wonder what happened to hers, and what happened to my wonderful new bike. I'm glad they put my seatbelt on. Otherwise I'd have slid over against that ugly cop when we went around that last corner.

The courthouse is beginning to look pretty familiar.

This time, there are more people standing on the sidewalk watching the cops drag me up the front steps. None of them are cheering, but some guy is shouting something that I can't make out. I'm again shoved roughly into the old elevator. I pray that the cable will break and we'll all drop into the basement and be killed. Doesn't happen. At the fourth floor they push me out the door and I walk down the hall, as well as I can with my ankles chained together.

The courtroom is packed and the hall is full of people too. The cops tell them that it's against fire code for them to stand in the hall. They'll have to go outside if there isn't any more room inside. I'm glad, because I don't want to walk down that crowded hall. I know they all hate me, and someone might try to kill me. After the hall clears out, we go inside. They take off my handcuffs and force me onto the seat beside Darrell. All three of them sit right behind us, ready to shoot me if they need to, I presume.

CHAPTER 60

The judge is finally announced and everyone has to stand while he strolls in acting like royalty. He shuffles through his papers while ignoring us commoners. Finally, he reads a paper that says what we're all here for, and then tells the prosecuting attorney to proceed with his opening statement.

Mr. Jacobs is still the prosecutor. He struts up front with his perpetual smirk firmly affixed to the front of his shiny bald head. Not only is he arrogant, he's also pretty long-winded. Unfortunately, I suspect that he's smart too.

"May it please the Court, and you, Ladies and Gentlemen of the jury." He starts off by describing the scene in the lunchroom in minute detail. He paints a vivid picture of me throwing my chair down, yelling vulgar insults at Todd, and screaming that I was going to smash his skull in.

"I think that you'll agree, after hearing the testimony of the witnesses to this violent outburst, that it was entirely unprovoked," he says. "Todd didn't even know the defendant. She could have chosen anyone to murder."

His description was so convincing that I almost believed him.

"I've got a hundred students who would gladly testify in Todd's behalf, but I've decided that in the interest of an expeditious trial, I'd only call on ten of them to testify. These ten are all girls. They all would be sympathetic to the defendant if they thought there were any possibility that she was being raped.

This all happened in the lunch room at noontime. Then, moving on to later in the afternoon, shortly after school, our three local football heroes had a rare break from the rigors of football practice because of the brilliance of their game against the Charlotte Eagles. They chose that peaceful interlude to take a leisurely ride out the Clark Brook road. A few miles from town, they observed the defendant. She was staggering around in the road and appeared to the boys, to be drunk. They thought she was in danger of being hit by a car, so they stopped to see if they could give her a ride home.

In the words of the two boys who survived the unprovoked attack, 'She had a vodka bottle in her hand and she reeked of liquor.' I might add that it was the same brand of vodka that her mother was addicted to."

"Objection. Irrelevant."

"Sustained. The clerk will please strike that last remark from the record. The prosecution will please confine their remarks to information that is pertinent to this case."

Mr. Jacobs continues. He got his little dig in about Mom anyway.

"When the defendant stumbled and almost fell, Todd bent down to grasp her arm in an effort to steady her. Upon seeing the opportunity to make good her threat and inflict the killing blow, she viciously attacked him with her liquor bottle. As you all well know, Todd Richardson died as the result of that violent unprovoked attack. However, we have two reliable witnesses, and their testimony will leave no doubt as to what happened that day or to the guilt of the defendant.

Given that the defendant has not chosen to plead insanity, I see no alternative. To prevent the possibility of another vicious, random attack, there is no other option. We must have the death penalty."

Mr. Jacobs smiles at the jury and struts back to his seat.

The judge says we're going to break for lunch before hearing the defense's opening statement. He instructs the jury to refrain from discussing what they've heard.

CHAPTER 61

A female cop brings me a baloney sandwich and a Coke. Then she escorts me to the bathroom while one of the male cops waits outside the door. By now I have no trouble peeing while someone's watching me. I'm pleased to note the new bathroom door and the much heavier mesh over the window. I've been instrumental in bringing about improvements to the old courthouse.

This lady cop acts as if she's afraid of me. If she thinks that I'm too close to her, she warns me to back off. All the while keeping her fingers wrapped tightly around the butt of her pistol. I suspect that she'd like to have the honor of shooting me. Women's equality and all that. They're all being very cautious. It's a matter of keeping the barn door securely locked, although the horse has already been stolen once. I don't know what they're worried about. My ankles are still chained together. I suppose if I wanted to, I could still randomly stage a vicious unprovoked attack on some unsuspecting innocent person.

The three cops sitting in the second row take turns going to lunch. That only leaves two of them, plus the lady cop, to shoot me if I get out of hand. I'd guess lunch hour is about two hours long. They wouldn't give me my watch back. I might use it as a lethal weapon.

Finally everyone files back into the courtroom. They pay homage to the judge, and the trial resumes.

"Defense may now present their opening statement."

"Thank you, Your Honor.

Ladies and Gentlemen of the jury, I regret to say that

I don't believe that you've yet heard what happened on the day that Todd Richardson was hit. There is one more reliable witness to the events of that day and her testimony will point out the errors in the story that you heard this morning. Miss Trent is innocent until it has been proven beyond any reasonable doubt that she is indeed guilty of murder, and that's going to be hard to do, because she is not guilty. I'm confident that you will reach a fair and just verdict, finding Miss Trent innocent. Thank you for your attention, and for your fair and unbiased decision after you have heard all the testimony and seen all the evidence."

Darrell's opening statement was much shorter than Mr. Jacobs's, but I think he did a good job. It's pretty discouraging, though. It's obvious just from looking at the expressions on people's faces that everyone's against him.

CHAPTER 62

The trial takes three days, which Darrell says is a very short time for a murder trial. Every afternoon, when they dump me back in my cell, it seems smaller. I can feel myself being worn down. Each night I lie on my bunk trying to think of something beautiful so that I can go to sleep. It doesn't really work anymore. I think I'll die before long even if they don't kill me.

The testimony of the ten girls is a long affair. Each girl spouts an almost identical spiel, describing an out-of-control demon, berating Todd, and promising to kill him. By now, I'm kind of in a fog. I'm probably really going to get the death penalty, which I've said is what I want. Faced with the fact that it's the most likely outcome, I'm not so sure. Let's face it, I'm scared out of my mind. North Carolina's method of execution is lethal injection, and I guess that's better than hanging, but you still end up dead.

I thought that Mr. Jacobs wouldn't really be able to prove something that wasn't true, but it appears that he can. Darrell comes up with some good arguments, but, the prosecution always has a better one. When Darrell said that I had nothing against Todd and even read the entry in my diary where I said that I thought he was great, Mr. Jacobs said that only proved his point. It was a random killing. I didn't choose my victims logically. No one was safe from me. He said I was new in this area, so this was probably my first victim here. He told the court that he'd checked back in Albuquerque where I came from, and couldn't find a criminal record there, but who knew how many people I'd killed and not been caught.

He said I'd have gotten away with it this time if there hadn't been witnesses.

When Darrell said that I'd been terrified when I hit Todd, and described how I'd escaped out the front door of the Navigator, Mr. Jacobs said he could picture me running down the road drunk, with my pants down around my ankles. He said the police had better be careful or I'd run off with the chain between my legs. Everyone had seen me come into the courtroom in chains and I was humiliated. Darrell objected and said that it hadn't been proven that I was drunk. The judge sustained the objection, but everyone had laughed at the picture Mr. Jacobs painted of me with my pants down. The damage was done.

Mr. Jacobs got in another low blow when he described in detail how I'd talked Grammy into driving me around even though she didn't have a license. He said I convinced her not to wear a seatbelt and hinted that I'd caused the accident so that I could collect the insurance. It made me so mad that I think I could have run over him with a dynamite truck.

Every day the two witnesses, Jason and Donny came to court with their football uniforms on. Between them was an empty chair with a number twelve uniform draped across it. Todd's uniform.

CHAPTER 63

By the time Mr. Jacobs makes his closing statement, I'm sure I'm going to die. I'm pretty depressed and I miss most of what he says. What I do hear sounds very convincing, though.

"There are over a hundred children who would have gladly given their testimony in this trial. That would have taken too much of your valuable time, and is entirely unnecessary. You've heard the testimony of twelve reliable witnesses. Ten girls, who would be sympathetic to the defendant if they thought there were any possibility of attempted rape. And these two boys. Ladies and gentlemen of the jury, you've known these boys for their whole lives. They were born and brought up right here among you. You've seen them grow up, pump gas, bag groceries, play football, and take your daughters to proms. Now, I ask you, would you take the word of a girl from away, whom you don't even know, over the sworn testimony of all of our own children? No! You must find the defendant guilty of first degree murder! Thank you."

There are more drawn-out court procedures taking place, but I don't really hear what's going on. This is as low as I've ever been in my life, and I'm starting to worry about me. In the past, I've been belligerent and defiant in my attitude toward the police and the court. Not anymore. Now I'm just scared. This is really happening. They are going to sentence me to death. I'm going to die. Thinking positive thoughts doesn't help at all. There isn't anything positive to think about.

The judge says something about adjourning until

tomorrow. I don't want to adjourn. I'm afraid to go back to that little cell. I think my mind is getting messed up. I've never felt this way before. I'm not sure, anymore, if my memories are real. I know Grammy was real because I can feel her necklace, and I know Mom was real because I have on the running shoes that she gave me. I'm not sure about my other memories, though. Maybe I really did do it.

CHAPTER 64

I have a hard time walking when the cops drag me out of the courtroom. I don't want to go back to my cell. It's too small. I'm even having a hard time getting in the elevator. I'm afraid of what they're doing to me, and what they're going to do to me.

The cops dump me on my cot, take off my irons, and then slam the door. It's too small in here. I can't breathe. I lay on my cot, not bothering to take my clothes off or get into bed. I try with all my might to think of something pretty, but I can't.

The guard comes with my supper, but I can't get up and take it from him. I'm not hungry anyway. When he stops telling me to take the tray and leaves, the cell gets even smaller. It's closing in on me and I can't breathe. I try to pray, but it feels as if even Jesus has deserted me.

I'm lying on my back on the tiny cot in my cell. Finally, I can do it. I pretend that I'm lying on my bed 'my bed' in Grammy's house. I stretch my arms and legs wide. I can't touch anything. There aren't any concrete walls. It feels too warm in here. I walk to the window and open it wide. The cool breeze washes over me while I look out at the forest behind the house.

All of a sudden, something happens to my mind. I'm not pretending anymore. I'm in the little clearing in the woods. It's an open space and I can smell the pine needles that I'm lying on. The little squirrel is perched on the branch above my face. If I don't move, he won't run up to the top of the tree, and I can stay here looking at him forever.

I'm in the dynamite truck with Jack and his

beautiful fiancée. They're laughing. The seat of the truck is a bench and I'm being strapped down. I can't move. I can't breathe. I'm dying.

I'm on the floor and it's dark. I'm surrounded by dark. I can't breathe. I get up and rush to the slot in the door. There's light in the hall, but there's no one there. I try to scream for help, but I can't breathe. My heart sounds like the engine in the dynamite truck. It's going too fast. I'm breathing really fast too, but it's not working. There's no air.

The guard...breakfast tray. I'm lying on the floor, holding Grammy's necklace. I'm sweaty and there's a big bump on my head. A pool of urine has soaked through my clothes. I've peed myself. The guard comes back with clean clothes and a package of wipes. No time for a shower. Police are here to take me to the courthouse. I strip off all my urine soaked clothes and sit on the little stainless steel toilet, completely naked. Using the wipes, I clean up as best I can. The cops are watching. I don't care. For some reason, I'm slow and awkward as I put my clean clothes on. I'm glad my running shoes and Grammy's necklace didn't get wet.

I feel weak; the cops have to practically drag me out to their cruiser. On the way to the courthouse, I think about going back to the cell after court. I can't do it. If I hurt myself, they'll have to take me to the hospital. Maybe I could get my arm caught in the toilet and break it, or stick it through the slot in the door and fall. That might break it. They might not be able to tell right away that it was broken, though, and they might just put it in a sling and put me back in the cell again anyway. I need a way to hurt myself that makes blood so they'll see it. I'll smash my face into the concrete wall of my cell. That will make lots of blood. It will mess my face up too, but I don't care. Everyone has always said how beautiful I am, but it hasn't done me much good so far. I think that will work. I'm not going to be able to stand being locked up in that cell again, no matter what it takes. When we get to the courthouse, there's a new fright. The elevator. It bothered me last time, but this time, I'm scared to death.

"Can't we please take the stairs?"

I'm sure that even if they hadn't had to carry me up the front steps, the cops would still have ignored me. They have to carry me into the elevator as it is. I can't go in there. It's too small. What if it gets stuck between floors? There wouldn't be any way out. I'd be trapped in there with no air to breathe. I have my eyes closed and I'm crying. It takes the tiny old elevator forever to get to the fourth floor. I'm going to have to get in it again to go back down, and then I'm going to have to go back to the cell.

CHAPTER 65

When I go into the courtroom, I feel like a mess. The cops have to almost carry me, and everyone is staring. They put me in the seat next to Darrell and I immediately lay my head on the table. While I'm waiting, I try to decide how to smash my face against the concrete. There has to be enough blood to get their attention. I should do it as soon as they take my chain off. That way they will see the blood and maybe they will take me to the hospital and not lock me in the cell. I can't stand when the judge comes in, but I try to listen. It's time for Darrell to convince the jury that I'm innocent. He has some good arguments, but Mr. Jacobs is right. There's no way the jury is going to believe me over the kids they know and have seen grow up.

It's finally over. I wonder how long it will be before my execution. I still have my head on the table. I can't help crying, but at least it's not loud.

The judge gives instructions to the jury. He tells them that a guilty verdict means that not one of them has a reasonable doubt that I'm guilty.

The people on the jury file out of the courtroom, and the judge announces that there will be a two hour recess. I guess he thinks that there's a good chance the jury will have already reached a verdict in two hours.

I see that some of the spectators are still in their seats when I'm escorted to the bathroom again. They don't want to take a chance on missing anything. I'm still crying a little and I try to wipe my face with my sleeve when I see that my teachers are here. Everyone else looks happy, but they all look sad, except for Mr.

Higgins. He's reading something. I always thought that maybe he liked me, but I guess he's not too concerned. When I get back to my seat, I put my head back down on the table again and close my eyes. I try to think of something beautiful, but it doesn't work. I'm still crying, but I just feel more numb than sad. Two hours is a long time. I wish I could go to sleep.

The judge was right. At the end of two hours, everyone including the jury, crowds back into the courtroom. When they have settled down, they all have to stand again while the judge comes in. I can't stand, and no one helps me. I just continue to sit with my head on the table and my eyes closed. I can't block out most of the words, but they don't mean anything. I'm still crying.

"Yes we have your honor."

"Guilty as charged on all counts."

"Reconvene in two days for sentencing."

"Prisoner to be remanded to county jail."

CHAPTER 66

I understood the last thing the judge said and I'm really crying now. I can't help it. I've got to go back to that tiny cell where I can't breathe. I don't pay much attention to what happens after that. I hear a few words, but they don't really register.

"Clerk

"Amicus Curiae

*"*Chambers.

The police start to pick me up to take me back, and I think I might pass out. I'll die when they put me back in that cell. I don't think I'll be able to smash my face hard enough.

Someone says, "Wait." The police put me back in my seat. I feel awful. I think I'm going to vomit for real. I put my head back on the table and try not to throw up. I don't know why we're waiting. That just puts it off. I'm grateful for the delay anyway.

"Miss Trent, come to chambers."

The cops behind me all jump up.

"Alone. And take those leg irons off."

I can't walk, so the bailiff helps me. The judge's room is too small and there are too many people. I can't go in there, but I have to. I close my eyes and the bailiff helps me. I'm crying.

"Miss. Trent, may I see the bottom of your sneaker?"

I can't hold it up, so Mr. Higgins helps me. Mr. Higgins? What's he doing here? I'm still blubbering when I talk to the judge.

"Judge, I'm sorry for being disrespectful. If it's

possible, I'd like to wear these running shoes that mom gave me and the necklace that Grammy gave me when I'm executed."

The judge just continues to look stern.

"Well, you're right. These sneakers have a large 'V' on the sole."

"Your Honor, I've been the phys-ed teacher in this school for a long time, and Vicky is the best athlete we've ever had. And that includes Todd Richardson. She is also very dedicated and a great kid. In my opinion, there's no way she could kill anyone on purpose."

The judge acts as if he doesn't hear any of it.

"Mr. Higgins. Would you please read that part of the attorney's notes again."

"Certainly."

"As they were putting me into the SUV, I got one leg free and pulled it back so that Todd couldn't get my pants all the way off. I kicked as hard as I could. My foot hit something solid and it pushed me all the way into the SUV."

"Miss Trent. Is that what happened?"

"Yes."

"This is highly unusual, but yes, as a friend of the court Mr. Higgins, you may ask one of the witnesses a question."

I'm led back to my seat. I'm still crying, but I hear some of what they're saying.

"Will Donald Gold please take the stand again."

"Do you realize that you're still under oath, Mr. Gold?"

"Yes."

"Donny, where did you get the bruise that I saw on your chest a few days after Mr. Richardson was struck?"

"I don't know. Football practice, I guess."

"We didn't have football practice for two weeks after the incident with Todd. Let me rephrase the question. Where did you get the bruise that matches Miss Trent's shoe print?"

I hear a voice that I recognize. Mr. Ames, the Gold's lawyer.

"Don't answer that question."

"The court directs Mr. Gold to answer the question."

I've got to get in the elevator again, then go back to the little cell. I put my head on the table again and try not to vomit. There is more talking and I hear someone else besides me crying, but none of it really registers.

"Murder one, dismissed. All the other charges punishable by time already served. The defendant is hereby free to go, with the apology of the court."

CHAPTER 67

When I wake up, I'm lying on a flat bench just like in the dream. I'm still crying, waiting for them to strap me down. It's a big room. I'm not back in my cell. Someone immediately walks up beside me. It's not a guard, it's a lady who looks like a real person.

"How do you feel?"

"Are you the one who gives the injections?"

"What injections?"

"You know, the lethal injections. Isn't that still how North Carolina executes people?"

"Honey, I'm a nurse. You're not going to get a lethal injection. Don't you know what happened in court? You're innocent."

She's crying now too.

"I am?"

"Yes."

"When do I have to go back to that cell?"

"Never."

***

It's been a month and I'm still in the hospital. I talk to a psychiatrist every day. Her name is Norma. She's really nice. She says that I've got problems, but that someday, I'll get better.

"By next week, you should be able to have company."

That's good, although I don't know of anyone who would come to see me. I've been doing a little reading and watching TV for the last few days, and time is passing more quickly than it did at first. I'm even sleeping with less medication. Maybe I *am* getting better.

In a few days, Norma brings up the visitor thing again.

"Okay, tomorrow you can have a visitor. You need to decide whom you want to see first."

"Is there really someone who wants to see me?"

"There are several people."

"I can't imagine who. Are you sure I'm up to it? I'm scared."

"You're up to it because you're strong. I know you must have had to face your fears before and you can do it again. It will be a very short meeting. Look at this list and choose the one that's going to be the hardest."

I'm surprised. There are a lot of people on the list. It's going to be hard to meet any of them, but I finally decide. I'm scheduled to meet with Mrs. Gold, who was once Amelia, the next day. I wonder if she'll really come.

I'm sitting alone in a room that's like a small living room, but not too small, when she comes in.

"Mrs. Gold, I'm so sorry that I deceived you. I shouldn't…."

"Hush child. How can we ever make amends for what we've done to you? Can you ever forgive me?"

"But I lied to you and took your money. I'm not even a painter."

You're a wonderful painter. You asked for my help and I ignored you. I don't think I'll ever be able to forgive myself."

"You had to believe in your son. That's what mothers are supposed to do."

"I could have at least listened to you and tried to check things out. We were all so sure that we were right."

"They say that someday I'll be well. I'm already sleeping better."

Mrs. Gold is crying as she kneels beside me and hugs me.

"I'm so sorry. You better hurry up and get better. I love you."

A bell sounds. Our time is up.

"I'll come back as soon as they'll let me."

She's crying when she leaves. My shrink sticks her head in the door.

"You okay?"

"Better than okay."

CHAPTER 68

Mrs. Gold visits me every day. She tells me that she's always wanted a girl and that I'm the most perfect girl she's ever known. Every time she leaves, she hugs me and tells me that she loves me.

Eventually, we get around to talking about Donny.

"He's in military school now. Staying here was too stressful. What he did was very wrong and his excuse was wrong too. He said that Todd had planned to rape you ever since you first came to school here. Todd has always been able to do anything he wanted to do, and he could tell that you weren't going to cooperate. His father is the police chief so Todd found out how to make contact with some pretty bad people. Donny said that he told him and Jason that he'd hired two of them to kill me and Jason's mother if they ever told. Donny said that he didn't know if it was true or not, but he couldn't take any chances. He said that Todd was really strange and he thought he'd be capable of doing something like that. Todd had a diary and Chief Richardson has already tracked down the people that Todd contacted, so we're safe now. Another reason that Todd couldn't say anything was that if he did, he'd be accused of participating in a rape. It was a terrible thing, but it's over. I just hope you get better in a hurry. We've still got your bike and your paints, and we still owe you for painting."

Norma, my shrink, is bugging me to meet with some of the others on the list of people who would like to see me. I agree to meet with Darrell to thank him and to ask him about Marie. We meet in the same room that I met

Mrs. Gold in.

"Hi Darrell."

"Hi Vicky. How are you?"

"Getting better all the time. Thank you for representing me when you knew that I was a lost cause."

"Vicky I'm really sorry. I was so busy that I didn't take the time to find out how much stress you were under. You should have been in the hospital."

"Well it's over now, and I'm getting better. What do you hear about Marie?"

"Marie's not doing very well. She has a cellmate who's a bully. I'm afraid for her, but there's nothing I can do. I don't represent her."

"Do you think she'd be eligible for parole?"

"I don't see why not. She certainly isn't a menace to anyone. She doesn't have bail money, though, or a place to stay when she gets out."

"Could you represent her?"

"Not unless the court appoints me, and that isn't going to happen."

I get up from the couch and walk to the window, scuffing my feet a little. At that prearranged signal, my shrink sticks her head in and announces that our time is up. I thank Darrell for coming, and wish him luck.

CHAPTER 69

Mrs. Gold has told me repeatedly that if there is anything that she can do for me, to just tell her. When she visits the next day, I take her up on her offer. I tell her all about Marie.

"She's only fourteen. She's not a criminal, she just can't make it on her own. I only knew her for a short time, but we were friends and I trusted her. She helped me escape. Do you think there's anything that you can do to help her?"

"Our attorney isn't a criminal lawyer, but I'll ask him what he can do. He usually does what I want if I push hard enough. I'll call him this afternoon and I'll let you know what he says when I see you tomorrow."

I know that the Gold's attorney is Stewart Ames, and he's on the list of people who want to see me. Besides representing the Golds, he was Grammy's lawyer. I wasn't impressed with his attitude when he called me while I was in jail, and I hope that Mrs. Gold will deal with him. If she does, I won't have to get involved.

When I see Mrs. Gold the next day, she seems excited.

"Stewart, I mean Mr. Ames our lawyer, says that he can get Marie out on bail if she can stay with me, but she can't be left alone. I can't be home all the time, but I've thought of the perfect solution. If you could come and live with me too, it would solve everything. What do you think?"

"I think it's a great idea and it's very kind and generous of you to suggest it, but I don't know if they will let me out of here. I *am* crazy, you know."

"You're not crazy. I can bring you in here for a meeting every day if they need to see you. I'm no psychologist, but I think it would be good therapy."

When I meet with Norma that afternoon, she isn't as enthusiastic.

"You've still got a way to go before you can be mainstreamed."

"I wouldn't be mainstreamed. I'd be staying with Mrs. Gold, and she said she'd bring me in every day to meet with you."

"You still have some issues."

"Like what."

"Sleeping, for one thing."

"I sleep okay."

"The night shift says you still scream in your sleep."

"I think they're exaggerating. I have woken up sweaty a few times, but I think even that is getting better, and I don't think I scream. Everyone has bad dreams once in a while."

"The night shift says that it's still every night."

"Well it's just because I don't get enough exercise. I'm not tired when I go to bed. I need to be where I can ride my bike and run. What else?"

"Well, you cry all the time."

"I don't cry all the time. I'm not crying now. I've always been emotional. What else?"

"You're very afraid of the police."

"Who wouldn't be? What else?"

"You're still very claustrophobic. You'd have a hard time dealing with tight places, for instance, elevators."

"I can't argue about that, but that isn't going to get

anyone killed. What else?"

"We're not worried about keeping anyone from being killed, we're worried about getting you well. There are a lot of little things, but we can work on them. I just don't think you're quite ready yet."

"Can you keep me here against my will?"

"I don't know. Don't you think that we're trying to do what's best for you?"

"It might surprise you, but no; I don't have a lot of faith that the people who have authority over me have my best interest at heart."

"I guess I had that coming. I do have your best interest at heart, though. Maybe in a week, two at the most, we could have a trial run for one night. Would that work for you?"

"Yes. If that's the best you can do."

"You see. You're making progress. You're trusting my judgment."

CHAPTER 70

The next person that I want to see, is Mr. Higgins. He was my gymnastics teacher, and also the man who saved me. We meet in that same little living room where I met Mrs. Gold and Darrell Jones. I know it's going to be an emotional meeting. When he walks in, I go over to him and hug him. I'm crying. Like Norma says, I've been doing a lot of that lately.

"You never told me that you liked me."

"I couldn't show favoritism, but you're definitely my favorite."

"It sure would have been nice to know that someone liked me. When I saw you reading in the courtroom, I thought you didn't care enough to pay attention."

"What did you think I was reading, the Wall Street Journal? I've been at a conference and I just got back. I should have stayed for three more days, but I came back for your trial. I was reading Darrell Jones's notes on your version of what happened. When I read what you said about kicking out and it pushing you into the car, the picture of Donny's bruise popped into my mind. I've always known that what they were saying about you couldn't be true. Are you trying to stay in shape?"

"There's no question that I owe my life to you. I can never repay you. I tried to exercise some while I was in solitary, but it's been quite a while since I've ridden my bike or run."

"Have you thought any about coming back to school? I've missed you and I know all your other teachers have too."

"Not really. You guys might not hate me, but

everyone else there does."

"Maybe, but I doubt it. People have probably changed their minds after finding out what really happened."

"I've missed so much school that I think I'd have to start this year over anyway."

"That's okay. I'd get to have you for an extra year."

By the time Mr. Higgins leaves, I feel a little more confident that I'm eventually going to get well. I know that Norma's right, though. I'm not there yet.

CHAPTER 71

Dear Diary,

I've missed writing to you. I'm doing it now for fun, not as a substitute for having friends. I have lots of friends now. We're on summer vacation from school, but lots of kids have made a real effort to befriend me. Doreen is still my friend, but she has lots of friends now too, and when school starts again in the fall, we won't be in the same grade. I missed so much school that I'm going to repeat last year. I'll be in the same grade as Marie. We're both staying with the Golds and she's my best friend. She says she'll help me with math.

Well, it's been three months since I spent my last night in solitary. That's the reference I use to judge time now. Not my birthday, Christmas, when I'll graduate, or any other landmark event.

That may sound depressing, or morbid, but I'm okay. I have a bedroom over the garage. A big bedroom. Everyone else has a bedroom on the other end of the house. That way, I don't disturb anyone. They tell me that I still scream in my sleep some, but not very often now, and I'm getting better.

I had a meeting with Grammy's attorney, Mr. Ames, two days ago and it went very well. He was extremely friendly. He said that he'd like to continue to manage my estate. He said that except for one-hundred thousand dollars that she left to the heart association, Grammy left everything to me. Everything being the house she lived in, a cattle ranch in California, and forty million dollars in other investments. Grammy even had a separate account to pay the inheritance taxes. He said that he'd been managing Grammy's affairs for a long time and that he'd send me a report showing how all my investments and properties have been preforming for the past ten years. He said that I have an interest bearing checking account with a million dollars deposited. It's hard to believe that I can just write out checks but I can. I tried it this morning, and it works. He gave me a card with his phone number and said that if I have any questions or problems, to call him, day or night.

I'd better sign off for now, but I'll try to write again tomorrow, or at least, as soon as I can.

Vicky

CHAPTER 72

I've met Jack and the beautiful girl that he's going to marry. Her name is Amy. I'm going to start painting, again, and the first painting I'm going to do is of them. It's going to be a wedding present. I hope they'll like it. I've always had fun painting and Norma says that it's good therapy. Mrs. Gold saved my painting stuff. Just in case, she said. I guess she wasn't completely sure that I was a murderer. She still has my portrait of her hanging in her foyer. I'm glad that she didn't throw it out when she found out about me.

I see Norma once a week now, mostly because she's a friend. The state won't pay for it anymore, but I like her and I can afford it.

I've been running and riding the bike that Grammy gave me. We got Marie a bike like mine and we're doing it together. I thought I was in bad shape, but Marie was terrible. I had a hard time talking her into going with me, but you should see her now. She still can't keep up with me running, but she's awesome on her bike. We're both getting in shape, and except for too much junk food, we're eating good too. Mr. Higgins says that we are going to start a track team this fall. He says that he doesn't know much about track and that I'll probably have to be the coach.

I still really miss Grammy. It helped a little when they gave me her personal effects. Although Grammy never wore jewelry, there *was* a tiny collection. Her engagement ring, wedding ring, and necklace.

Someone's knocking on my bedroom door. My bedroom is over the garage and I practically never have company up here. When I open the door, Mrs. Gold is standing on the landing at the top of the stairs.

"Can I come in?"

"Of course."

"I heard that you were painting a picture of Jack and Amy."

"Yes, it's going to be a wedding present. Who told you? It's supposed to be a secret."

"Oh, a little birdy named Marie. That should be a great present. I thought I'd come up and see how it's progressing. Does it make you nervous to have people watch you paint?"

"Not you. I'm really just getting started. All I've done so far is make a rough outline. I'm sorry that my room's such a mess."

"Your room isn't a mess. Have you been in Marie's room?"

"Not lately."

"Well, her room's a disaster. You were right, though. She's a great kid and I love her."

"I do too."

"Another reason that I came to see you is to ask you if you could finish the painting on Jack's truck before you get too involved in this one. I'll understand if you don't want to go back to the garage. Maybe Jack could park his truck somewhere else."

"That might be less stressful right now, but sure, I'd like to finish it."

"Good, I'll talk to Jack and let him decide where to park it long enough for you to finish."

"It should only take me about an hour or so."

"Could you do it now if Jack is free?"

"Sure."

"Can I borrow your cellphone? I'll call him right now."

Mrs. Gold talks to Jack for a minute, then gives my phone back.

"He's going to park his truck in a gravel pit, then he and Amy will come here in her car and pick you up. He doesn't let anyone ride in his truck."

"Too late. I already have."

"I know."

CHAPTER 73

I'm sitting in a lawn chair on the landing in front of my room when Jack and Amy drive up in an older blue Camry. She's driving.

"Hi Vicky."

"Hi Amy. Hi Jack."

Jack doesn't have his usual brilliant smile. I wonder if something's wrong. I have my painting things in a little case that Mrs. Gold gave me. I climb in the back.

"I've seen some of your paintings. You're really good. That one of Mrs. G almost looks alive."

"Thanks Amy."

Every time Amy sees me, she tells me how sorry she is for what happened to me, and how smart she thinks I must be for not getting caught for so long.

"Escaping in Jack's truck was brilliant. You're one spunky kid."

Jack isn't saying anything. It's a short ride to the gravel pit where Jack parked his dynamite truck. It's warm enough to have the windows down, but not warm enough to run the air conditioner. When we get to the gravel pit, I ask Jack if he will turn the truck around so the door that I'm painting will be in the shade.

"Sure."

He moves the car over by the bank of the pit, away from the truck.

"You guys stay over here in the car while I turn the truck around."

After he walks back to the truck, Amy says, "He's really safety-conscious. I guess in his job you have to be. He doesn't want anyone else near his truck when he's moving it. It must be dangerous to be near it, but he's driving it. He must know what he's doing, but I still worry about him."

After the truck is turned around, I wait a few minutes for it to cool off after being in the sun, then I start painting. They watch me for a few minutes, and then go back and sit in the car. They're parked in the curve of the wall of the gravel pit, and the sound is focused to the spot where I'm painting. I can hear every word they're saying. At first, I'm embarrassed. I wonder if I should tell them. Then, I feel bad. They're fighting. I have to listen. How can such a perfect couple be fighting?

"We helped him pay back the Golds last time. Now he's twenty-two thousand in debt again. He's sick. His gambling isn't just ruining *his* life; it's ruining ours too."

"I know all that, but he's my brother. What do you want me to do, abandon him?"

"I want you to think of us for a change. We've worked hard for what we have. You're already giving up a fancy wedding so we can put a down payment on a house, and now you want to give all our savings to him. That won't cure him either. He won't even admit that he's sick. I know he's your brother, but I just can't do it again."

"You know these people he owes are bad news. He could end up with broken bones, or even be killed. I just can't let that happen."

"Well at some point, he's going to have to face the consequences of his actions, and it might as well be now, before he bankrupts us."

"You know that after our folks died, all we had was each other. I've always been able to rely on Roger. I just can't let him down now."

"Well maybe he's all you need to rely on now. I think we should put our marriage on hold until we sort things out. If we aren't going to get married, I don't care what you do with our money."

I feel sick. After I finish the painting, Jack drives the truck away without saying anything. I get in the car with Amy. She's crying and very soon, I am too.

"I heard you arguing," I confessed.

"That darned Roger. He's ruining my life. I love Jack. I can't believe this is happening."

"Does Roger work?"

"Yes, He works at the Ford garage. He's a good mechanic and he's reliable. He just has a gambling problem."

"He can't pay off his debt with what he earns?"

"No. Those people want their money now. He borrowed money from the Golds last time and wasn't very prompt at paying it back. We helped him out last time and some of his friends did too. No one who knows him will lend him money now. Of course the bank would lend him money to buy a new car but no one's going to help him out of this mess. He's just not responsible." When Amy drops me off, she's still sniffling a little. I feel terrible too.

CHAPTER 74

It's five o'clock and after talking with Amy, I'm really upset. I ride my bike into the Ford garage driveway with a sign over it that says 'Service Department' in big blue letters. It's quitting time, and someone is walking out of the little door on the end of the building.

"Can you tell me where I can find Roger?"

I don't even know his last name. Not very good planning. One of my spur-of-the-moment ideas. It's better to be lucky than smart, though.

"He's right behind me. Wears cowboy boots."

When he comes out, I walk up to him. He looks a lot like Amy. Same black hair, same eyes. Women must love him. He's a pretty nice-looking guy.

"Can I talk to you for a minute?"

He looks me up and down.

"Anytime you want, honey. How old are you?"

"Where can we talk?"

"My car's right over here."

He starts walking toward the parking lot.

"What's this all about, sweet thing?"

I don't say anything until we're seated in a fancy Mustang.

"I like Amy."

He doesn't say anything, but the expression on his face darkens noticeably.

"You know, your sister, Amy. She and Jack are fighting because of you. They're even thinking of calling off their wedding."

"And this is your business because?"

He's scowling now. Not so pretty anymore.

"I have time invested in their wedding, and besides, like I said, I like Amy."

"You just talking, or have you got something to say?"

Clearly, he doesn't want me sticking my nose in his business.

"How much is it going to take to get the wolf off your back?"

"Twenty-two thou."

He doesn't like me, except for the way I look, but at least he's being up front.

"How long have you got?"

"Saturday."

"Can you call them?"

"Yes. Why would I?"

"If I could arrange to cover the debt, would you agree to see a shrink two times a week for six months at my expense?"

He thinks about it for a minute, which is probably a good sign.

"I guess so, but if pigs could fly, I'd hitch a ride to Hawaii."

"Offer them five thousand a month for five months."

"And where am I going to get that?"

"Just see if they'll deal."

Roger whips out his fancy cellphone and calls.

"They'll take fifteen now and fifteen in a month."

"Tell them fifteen now and five a month for four months. Final offer."

"They heard you and they say 'deal.' "

"Yes, I know what day it is."

"I know. Saturday."

He hangs up and just stares at me.

"Good," I say.

"Oh sure. And where are we going to get fifteen?"

"What's your last name?"

"Sanford."

I take out my check book and write out a check. I hold it out, but out of his reach.

"There are conditions. You tell Amy that your problem is solved. You are through gambling. You have a legit backer, and you tell her what the conditions are. You do not say who your backer is. Also make her promise not to bail you out if you ever get in trouble again.

If you miss an appointment with the shrink, or if you gamble at all, it's over."

I hold out the check to him, and he takes it.

"Write your address and phone number on the back of my checkbook."

I hand him my pen and checkbook.

"Fifteen."

"Fifteen?"

"You asked me how old I was."

I get out of his car.

After Roger drives off, I call Norma's emergency number. I get voice mail.

"I hope you've got a couple of open appointments a week for the next four months. If you don't, you can use mine."

CHAPTER 75

Amy and I have become friends. Since her problems with Roger have been resolved, she's a happy upbeat person again and I like being around her. She's been good for me. She has even talked me into using the elevator at Macy's and I can do it on my own now.

I've finished painting the picture that's going to be my wedding present to her and Jack. It's hidden in my closet so she won't see it when she pays me a visit. Right now, I'm working on a portrait of Mr. Gold.

"Hi Vicky."

"Hi Amy. Come on in."

"I see you're painting Mr. G."

"Yes. He thinks I'm mad at him for calling the cops on me, and I want to give it to him to show him that I'm not."

"Well, I think you're mad at me too," she laughs.

"I'll just have to paint something for you too. What are you doing today?"

"I've got the day off, and I'd like to pick up Mrs. G's car. The Golds have been really good to Jack and me."

"They've been really good to me too. When are you going?"

"I'd go right now, but I have to wait for Jack to take me over to get it."

"Where is it?"

"It's at that new car wash. She took it in there to get it detailed."

"I could drive your car back, if that's all you need."

"You don't have a license."

"Grammy Albert drove for years without a license, and besides, Norma tells me that I have to get over my fear of cops."

"Who's Norma?"

"She's my shrink. It would be good therapy. Anyway, what's the worst thing that could happen? They don't execute kids for driving without a license, even in North Carolina."

"Can you drive?"

"Ask Jack. I drove his dynamite truck."

"Okay, let's go."

When we get to the car wash, Amy gets the keys, slides into the driver's seat of the big Lincoln and starts back to Mrs. Gold's house. I follow her in her Camry.

CHAPTER 76

Well, I really am being pulled over by a cop. His blue lights are flashing. I had to stop at a red light that Amy made it through. She has gone ahead in Mrs. Gold's car. I'm all alone and there's a cop walking up behind me. I'm scared. My first impulse is to mash the accelerator to the floor and try to get away, but somehow, I don't. He has his little book out. Maybe he'll just give me a summons and not arrest me and take me to jail. I know they aren't going to put me back in solitary for being too young to drive, but I'm not thinking rationally. In spite of acting so brave in my discussion with Amy, I'm panicked. I do manage to roll my window down. The cop looks at me through his sunglasses. I can't see his eyes, but I recognize that jagged scar to the left of his mouth. I have the heart rate of a hummingbird who thinks the cat has caught him.

"Oh...You've got a brake light out. Have a good day Miss Trent."

He stuffs his little book back in his pocket, walks back to his car, pulls out around me, and drives away. I just sit there stunned for about five minutes before I can drive on. I'm all shaky. That cop is one of the ones who had their pistols pointed at my head. He knows I'm fifteen and don't have a license. Maybe they aren't all as hard as I thought.

CHAPTER 77

Dear Diary,

I'm sorry I haven't been writing, but I've just been too busy. I had to write and tell you about the big game, though, but first I'll tell you what's been happening. Marie and I moved into Grammy's house. I thought living with the Golds would be too awkward when Donny came home for a visit. He's seeing a shrink now too, by the way. Either Amelia, Mrs. Gold, or Amy visits us at least a couple of times a week. They say they miss us, but I think there's another reason too. There are a lot of cute boys at school and they want to make sure that none of them follow us home.

Marie and I exercised and ran almost every day all summer. By fall, we were in awesome shape. I've grown some. I'm five five now and weigh a hundred and fifteen. Marie's still five feet two. Because of us, our basketball team is the smallest in the state. Guess who's the biggest. You guessed it. The

Charlotte Eagles. That's who we played for the state championship. They are a big school, but we were both undefeated in our class. I hate to brag, but Marie and I won the game. She was deadly under the basket. She's so small that they couldn't control her without fouling. She can hit the long ones too. I kept stealing the ball and feeding it to her and she got thirteen three pointers. Besides that, she never missed a foul shot. The Eagles played a good game, but we still won by six points.

The game was in Charlotte, but I think our whole town was there. Jack and Amy are married now and they were there cheering us on. When the game was over, it looked as if the bleachers on our side of the stadium just dumped their contents onto the floor. A bunch of people that we don't even know, picked Marie and I up and carried us around. We sure feel as if we belong here now.

I'm a junior again and so is Marie. She's only fifteen, but she's really smart. She got me straightened out on math in a hurry. I painted a beautiful picture of her, and she sent it to her folks in Cuba. She, Amy, and I are going to visit them on spring vacation. Next summer, we're all going to check out my ranch in California.

If anything else that's interesting happens, I might write again.

Vicky

gwheaton@rivah.net